BREAK
THE ICE

PIPER RAYNE

Cover design: RBA Designs

Line Editor: Love N Books

Proof Reader: Shawna Gavas, Behind The Writer

The Winter Games are over, but the bedroom games are just beginning…

This is about the time I normally hang up my snowboard and chill for a while. Except this year. This year, I'm dealing with what fate dealt me at the Winter Games— nope, not gold. A broken arm.

Since I'm not close to my family, I head to my best friend, Skylar's pad to recoup. Turns out having your gorgeous, single, sexy friend wait on you hand and foot can blur the lines between friendship and romance.

Which is exactly why I've decided to help her find a boyfriend.

Yeah, you heard me right. I'm going to help her comb through every dating app available until she finds the perfect man. What else could remind me of my place in her life more than watching her fall for someone else?

I can deal. I'm used to pushing through pain. I'm an Olympian after all.

BREAK THE *Ice*

To those who have the guts to risk friendship for love.

Note to Readers: *We used Winter Classics instead of the trademarked names Winter Games and/or Olympics. We did take a few creative liberties as well.*

CHAPTER ONE

S ometimes you just know whether a person is worth committing your time to without ever exchanging a word. It could be the briefest encounter or strictly observational. Do they say thank you to a cashier when receiving their change? Hold the door open for the person behind them? Do they *take* a penny from the jar or *add* a penny?

People can be shitty. I'm not going to dive into my horrible childhood or how I probably had it rougher than most. I hate pity more than I hate the Swiss. Relax, the snowboarders, not the actual Swiss people.

Back to my point—people who say they get duped or mislead by someone just aren't as bright at dissecting people's non-verbal cues. Take for instance the first time I met Skylar Walsh.

I was at a bar with my new teammates Grady and Dax. Each of them checked her out when she walked through the door alongside a few other skiers. The team was at a promo event and being the new kid around the circuit, I didn't know a lot of people.

"Ugh, Demi Harrison." Dax downed the rest of his beer. "I'm surprised she'd lower her standards and come here."

The bar was a rundown ski bar meant for warming the blood in your veins with mass amounts of alcohol. Everything was made of wood and the place was dim, but I kind of liked it. It was a homey place.

"She's cute," I said about the girl with long auburn hair piled up on her head and green eyes that seemed to glow when she talked to her friends. Truth was, she wasn't just cute, she was hot. But it wasn't Demi who caught my eye first. The brunette at her side with a million-dollar, welcoming smile that felt like the hot summer sun piercing my heart.

"Dax approached her once...didn't go well." Grady leans back in his seat, his usual scowl on display. I'm not even sure I've seen the guy smile since I met him two months ago. I heard his friend, Brandon Salter, had an accident and fucked Grady's psyche up. I've learned enough from my past to keep my mouth shut. This wasn't my first rodeo being the new kid. You wait for people to invite you into their drama, you don't go searching for it.

"What about the girl who's with her?" I asked and neither of them said anything.

"Skylar Walsh," Grady finally said. "Skier." He tipped his drink back, motioning to the bartender to bring him another.

I took their silence afterward to mean she didn't have a reputation, which was more than intriguing to me. I watched her as I sat with my new friends. She had a contagious smile on her face, her hands moving a mile a minute while she told them some story that made the girls' heads tip back in laughter. She didn't hog the attention, and when her friend said something she listened, her one hand constantly touching her friend's forearm. Her eyes weren't glued to her phone, but instead, her undivided attention was fixed to whatever her friends were saying.

The waitress came by, and like her friends, she said hello, used the waitress' name, gave her order and said thank you. She said thank you when the waitress set down her drink, too, with eye contact. In this day and age, that was almost unheard of. But that's not what drew me to her.

We continued to drink, well, Grady and I. Dax had been up and down chatting with a few guys and girls. I swear the guy knew everyone. Well, Grady did too, but unlike Skylar, he grunted when people said hi and patted him on the back with what always looked like sympathy in their eyes.

When Skylar and Demi left the bar and it was still wicked cold outside. The wind had kept us from boarding all day. They bundled up, zipping their jackets up to their noses and putting on hats and gloves before leaving. Demi walked out first, holding the door open for Skylar. Skylar walked through as small of an opening as she could and then pressed on the door to get it closed quicker so a rush of cold air wouldn't hit the patrons of the bar.

I was floored. Maybe it's nothing to some people, too minute to notice, but to me, that said something about what type of person she was. I've met a lot of *creeps, even more bitches in my life. Skylar Walsh was as nice and considerate as they come and wouldn't fuck me over. I ignored the tightness in my pants, ignored the beauty she laid bare for everyone to see because I was sure she wasn't a girl you could mix sex and friendship with, and at this point, a trustworthy friend was ten times better than a random one-night stand.*

Now, as I sit on her couch four years later, I wonder where that Skylar went.

She pops her head in a minute later and tosses a bottle of water across the room to me. I'm going to ignore the fact that I think she may have been aiming at my head. "Where did my nice nurse go?" I ask, my ass on the couch, my feet on an ottoman, my arm in a sling with some newly inserted pins to keep my bones company.

"Nice nurse left when you turned into a wimpy self-entitled whiner. Man up, Myers." She sits back down at the kitchen table in front of her laptop.

I'm staying at her parents' place in Chicago while my arm heals. They're in Arizona, thank goodness. I love them, they treat me like a son, but after the Classics, I need a little space from family time.

"Well, I'm sorry, but I did break my arm—saving your ass. Is a little compassion too much to ask?"

She narrows her eyes and pulls her long dark hair into a messy ponytail, tucking the strands too short to fit in the elastic behind her ears. This go-to move tells me she's taking off her gloves and we're about to go a few rounds. Unable to do anything fun and being secluded with her in her childhood home isn't what I'd planned after the Classics and I'm getting a little stir crazy.

"So, you'd rather I broke my arm?"

I should've just watched a movie.

"A measly thank you isn't hard."

Her hands move up in the air, she mumbles something to herself and then her hands ball up into fists. "I'm not going to baby you, Beck. I brought you to my parents' house to recoup after your surgery because I love you and you're my friend. Don't make me regret my decision." Without even waiting for me to respond, she directs all her attention back to her computer and the damn applications to grad school that are more important than me.

Where did that sweet girl who shut the door so strangers wouldn't get cold go?

"Maybe I should just go to a hotel." I pretend to sit up, wiggling my way up since I only have the use of one arm.

An annoyed stream of obscenities floats out of her mouth.

"You should be happy your nieces aren't here."

She grabs her computer, walks over to the couch and sits down next to me, her sock covered feet landing next to mine. I bump my foot with hers. Nothing. I do it again. She side glances me. Third time is the charm and when she looks over, she's fighting a smile.

"Sorry, I do appreciate you playing nursemaid." I swing my good arm around her shoulders.

She lightly jabs me in the stomach. "I know it's hard on you."

That's why Skylar and I get along so well. A girlfriend would've pretended to be upset forever just so I had to have flowers delivered or something. Shit rolls off Skylar's back as fast as it does mine. Life is way too short to let crap like that eat away at you.

"Don't use the hotel thing again." Her dark eyes narrow.

I chuckle, pulling her closer and kissing the top of her head. "How are the applications going?"

She shrugs.

"What about skiing?" I ask.

I thought Skylar was like me. We'd try to stay on the US ski and snowboarding team until we broke something unfixable or we didn't make it one year. Now she's talking about grad school. The kicker being she's looking at coming back to Chicago permanently. She'd go from being a mile away from me to what? Thousands, I guess. Math and geography are not my strong suit. Flipping through the air after flying off a ramp and landing on my feet? I'm an honor roll student.

She chews on the inside of her cheek. "I'm not sure I have another four years of training and committing to the sport on that level in me. Plus, age isn't on my side."

"You're twenty-five," I deadpan.

Her fingers type away. Skylar was different than most of us. She got her college degree while still skiing, which shows how much more of a go-getter she is than yours truly.

High school was enough for me and I tend to not think about my future. Think of it as an extra present you get when you're a foster kid—no time is guaranteed so you're just happy when you get through the day. It really is a one day at a time existence.

"You're practically a baby, Sky."

Her eyes are still fixed on the computer and I can see that I've lost her attention as she prepares for the future.

For me, the future is like dark clouds looming in my peripheral vision while there are still blue skies above. It's there and I know it's coming, but sometimes I close my eyes and let the sun shine down on me. Ignorance really is bliss, so whoever came up with that quote should be challenging Bill Gates for the smartest guy in the world title. I'm sure there are smarter guys than Bill Gates, but the hell if I know their names.

Skylar probably does.

"What did you say?" She looks over at me briefly before her gaze moves back to the computer screen.

Is that a rumble of thunder I hear in the distance?

CHAPTER TWO

"It's nothing I haven't seen before." Skylar breezes into the bathroom, doing her hair as I sit in a tub that took literally twenty minutes to get into. Okay, a slight exaggeration, but with a broken arm, sitting in a bathtub is about as easy as wrestling a pig in a pile of tar.

The downside of her parents' house is that there's only one bathroom. Yep, who has one bathroom nowadays?

"You should buy your parents a house with two bathrooms." I lean forward, pulling the shower curtain so that only my top half is exposed. Skylar has seen my dick, but not in the way your dirty mind is thinking. Let's just say, this isn't our first time nursing the other one back to health. I've seen her tits too. Well, some serious side boob anyway. But not her downstairs though, she's always very skittish with that.

She stops moving the eyeliner pencil across her lid and balks at me. "Sure thing, right after I pay for grad school. Remember, bronze medal here." She raises her hand. I hate the way she acts like bronze is runner-up for homecoming queen. I haven't said so, but I have my suspicions that it's part of the reason why grad school seems like such a great option for her right now.

"Bronze is killer," I say, watching her in the mirror. She wears too much makeup. She's prettiest when she's out on the ski hill with flushed cheeks and no make-up on.

"Says the silver medalist."

"Sky, you gotta give yourself a break. Look how many people went home with nothing."

She rolls her eyes before applying her eyeshadow. More shit to cover her girl-next-door face. I'm wasting my breath fighting her on this issue. I've been where she is during the last Classics when I didn't medal at all. It sucks, but quit? No way. That isn't me and it isn't Skylar. She thinks she'll be happier here, in Chicago without a mountain in sight, but I'm certain that's not the case.

"Do you have any decent places to ski around here?"

"Not really. Wisconsin and Michigan have a few, but they're not like the mountains."

Maybe my geography isn't that bad. I knew there were no mountains around.

"What are you going to do if you're in grad school and the itch comes? Drive to Wisconsin and ski the bunny hill?"

Her eyeshadow case shuts and she leans her hip against the counter. "Stop trying to sway me."

I raise the hand on my good arm out of the water. "I'm just helping you think every possible scenario through."

She turns and starts applying another layer of crap she doesn't need. She's quiet for a minute and then says, "I'm going to come see you."

"You make it sound like your decision is made already."

"It's not, Beck. I know you're worried and you don't want any space between us." She stuffs all her makeup into a bag and sits on the toilet, looking at me intently. "Nothing will change between us, just the amount of physical distance."

Distance changes everything.

She grabs the garbage bag I'm supposed to have on my arm, falling to her knees on the tile floor beside the tub and wrapping my arm. "You can't get this wet. Why didn't you put it on?"

"Kind of hard with one arm." I shrug my good shoulder.

"That's why I'm here. To help."

She glances around for a rubber band, but that snapped two days ago, so she pulls her ponytail out, her hair falling over her shoulders like one of those shampoo commercials. My eyes stay trained on her hair, wondering what it would feel like to run my fingers through it, but that's not happening.

I have a list of things I refuse to do because it only increases the chances of overstepping that delicate line between friendship and ending up with nothing at all.

"In that case, can I get a sponge bath?"

She smacks me lightly on the back of my head. "You shut the shower curtain, so I wouldn't see your penis, but you want a sponge bath?"

"I'm in the middle of a dry spell."

She laughs, standing to her feet.

"Wash my hair?" I ask before she sneaks out of the room.

She walks back in immediately. "Fine."

Kneeling back down to the linoleum floor, I slide up in the tub and bring my head back, making it easier on her to reach my head and easier for me to hide my package.

She squeezes shampoo into her hands, lathering it up and then moves her fingers along my scalp. Her gentle hands work my hair better than any hairdresser and I close my eyes at the peaceful feeling that engulfs me.

Neither one of us says anything, but she doesn't rush the job. Using her niece Molly's hair bucket thingy, she dips it in and pours it over my head, still using her fingers to help the water rinse the suds out. Her breast rubs against my arm and a zillion bolts of something that feels like electricity head straight to my dick. Skylar Walsh's breast has grazed my arm more times than the Pope has said a Hail Mary. So, why does my dick decide that right now is the time to react? I try to shift a bit, but it's useless. There's no concealing the fact that it's sprouting out of the water like a fucking whale surfacing.

Maybe a sponge bath wasn't such a good idea.

Her hands work faster, and I bring my knees up, hoping like hell she can't see it. When she finishes, my body already yearns to keep her with me, but she stands, drying her hands on the towel. "If you need help getting out, holler."

Did she feel the energy shift, too?

"I'll be good, thanks."

She says nothing, and I hear her footsteps descending the stairs. Thank goodness. I'll be in peace with my erect dick to dry off.

I slide back, resting my arm on the side of the tub, my head leaning back on the warm tile. Closing my eyes, my brain is anything but calm. Maybe it's the injury messing with my mojo.

I hear the front door open, small footsteps running in and then the door slam closed again.

"Aunt Sky! Aunt Sky!" her nephew Caiden yells.

"Auntie Sky!" Molly screams.

Shit. Zoe and her kids are here.

"Hey guys." Skylar's probably bending down to swoop them up. Her niece and nephew are her world.

"Where's Beckett?" Zoe asks.

Shit. Skylar left the door open. I search for anything to throw over myself. The towels are too far away and unless I want to yank the flowery shower curtain that Mrs. Walsh told me she hand made when the kids were younger—long and boring story—I'm shit outta luck.

Using my good arm, I push up on the tub, grunting as I struggle to gain my footing.

"He's upstairs. He'll be down in a second."

The footsteps blazing a trail up the stairs are as fast as my heart beats. I use all my arm strength to shut the door.

"No!" Molly screams on the other side of the door.

"You two sit. Uncle Beckett will be down in a second," Skylar says, obviously having followed them upstairs.

I let out a relieved breath, slowing my movements so I don't break a leg or my other arm.

I can hear Skylar and Zoe yammering on and on about the Classics and their parents being in Arizona and how the parents of Zoe's husband, Vin, insisted she bring over some rumaki.

I always did love Zoe's in-laws.

The sound of foil opening has my ears pricking because those two little piglets are going to eat all the delicious water chestnuts wrapped in bacon. My stomach growls. This is the best part of the Classics being over. I can eat whatever I want.

My steps over to the towel rack become more urgent since I know that by the time I dry off and get dressed with the use of one arm, the rumaki will be gone.

I reach toward the towel rack with my good arm while I'm standing in the tub and the small embroidered towel falls to the ground. I should've asked Skylar to bring my towel closer. Finally, with both feet out, I inhale another breath and set my gaze to the towel, mentally prepping to retrieve it.

Hell, maybe I'll go downstairs in a towel, steal some rumaki, and then get dressed.

Grabbing the towel, I realize I have to get dressed first because without the use of my other hand, I can't wrap it around myself. *Motherfucker.*

I take the corner of the towel, letting it hang open, rumaki at the forefront of my mind as I look down and try to figure out a way to swing the towel around my waist and somehow catch it with my good hand.

"AHHHHH!" a piercing scream echoes through the small space.

My head whips up and my gaze flies to the open door. Four-year-old Molly is standing there wide-eyed and staring at my junk.

Fuck!

I hurriedly place the towel over me, scrunched up with one fist but covering all the important parts.

Caiden crawls like an army guy behind her up the stairs.

"Molly?" Zoe's panicked voice rings throughout the house.

"I'll be right out." I shut the door, my heart hammering in my chest with an unnatural rhythm, my breath hiccupping from the adrenaline of a little girl seeing me stark naked.

Four footsteps stomp upstairs. "Molly, I told you to stay downstairs."

"Sorry, Mommy, I wanted to surprise Uncle Beckett."

My back slumps against the door.

"Next time listen to me, okay? You probably scared Uncle Beckett." Zoe's voice is ten decimals calmer now.

"Mommy," Molly says. "Did you know that Uncle Beckett's penis is *way* bigger than Caiden's?"

You could hear a pin drop in that hallway.

"We talked about this, Molly. Boys have penises and girls have vaginas. And size doesn't matter anyway, sweetie."

"Yeah," Caiden says all smug.

"Since when?" Skylar asks and snickers.

I can imagine her sister shooting her a death glare. A second later, I hear Caiden squealing and telling his auntie to swing him around again.

"I know, but it was kind of scary looking."

Skylar and Zoe bust out laughing and I close my eyes shaking my head. I'm never going to live this down.

CHAPTER THREE

I head downstairs, dressed in track pants and a t-shirt. At least I've mastered the art of putting my injured arm in first and tossing it over my head. I guess I'm more limber than I thought.

The house is silent, and I suspect Molly and Caiden are downstairs, Molly probably giving her brother a complex at his young age since it's practically Darwinian for boys to want everything big.

Rounding the bottom of the staircase in Skylar's parents' home, I spot the sisters at the table, picking up the rumaki and laughing over what just happened.

How do I ever look Molly in the eyes again?

"Thanks for that, Zoe." I grab a soda out of the fridge and join them at the table, pulling the aluminum pan full of rumaki in front of me.

"Well, if I'd known you were giving away peep shows, I'd have strapped her to the chair to keep her down here." Zoe props one foot up on the chair, swinging her long brunette hair around to one side.

It's apparent the two are sisters on the outside, but Zoe

is more aggressive than Sky. Maybe it's a momma bear thing, but I always feel like I teeter on the edge of whether or not she'll go off on me.

"If I'd known I was giving away peep shows, I would've made sure the spectators were old enough to vote."

"She'll forget it by tonight." She waves me off, leaning over the table and stealing a rumaki.

"Long enough for Vin to kick my ass."

She laughs. "Nah, he'll understand. Molly doesn't get privacy. Vin just moves faster than you."

Sky rolls her eyes, using a toothpick to grab another rumaki.

I cover it with my hands. "These are mine. Made for me."

"Well, until Mrs. Shapiro finds out you flashed her granddaughter." Zoe's eyebrows shoot up.

I push the pan back into the middle of the table. "I'm eating too much anyway."

They each waste no time continuing to consume all the food.

"Mommy." Molly stops in her tracks when she sees me at the table.

Zoe's eyes shift to me and then back to her daughter. "It's okay, Molly. Uncle Beckett has pants on."

Skylar throws a toothpick at her sister. "Come here, my favorite niece." She opens her arms wide.

"I'm your only niece," Molly deadpans, too smart for her own good.

Molly slides up on her aunt's lap anyway, sure to avoid making eye contact with me.

"Why don't we apologize to Uncle Beckett for walking in on him," Skylar whispers loud enough that we can all hear.

Molly peeks up through the long dark eyelashes she inherited from her mother.

I smile and roll my eyes.

She giggles.

"I'm sorry," she says, her voice soft and low.

I pick up a piece of the rumaki with a toothpick and hold it out to her.

"But Nana made them for you." She's yet to pick up her head.

I look around at the pile of toothpicks in front of Skylar and Zoe. "For you, I'll always share." I wink. She takes it from my hand, biting conservatively at first. "How about you do a drawing on my bandages?"

Her eyes widen, popping the entire bacon wrapped water chestnut into her mouth and running out of the room to their designated play area when they're here.

"Chew, Molly," Zoe screams after her daughter.

A minute later Molly returns, her cheeks still puffed out with the food, but she's got her markers, sliding into the chair next to me. "Let me see it."

I remove the sling carefully and hold out my arm and she uses it as her own personal canvas while we eat rumaki.

And as quick as that, the whole bathroom incident is forgotten.

***

"WILL you stop putting crap in the cart." Skylar picks up the pack of Oreos and puts them back on the shelf.

"You're being a killjoy." I toss in some Chips Ahoy anyway.

"Hey, Mr. Silver Medalist, you may be able to sit your

ass on the couch for a few months, but the rest of us have to keep in shape."

I stop, turning around, stopping the cart with my good hand. She falters back, her eyes wide in surprise.

"So, no grad school?" I ask.

Her shoulders slump and she shakes her head a few times. "I haven't decided yet, but if I want to continue to ski, Chips Ahoys aren't going to help me spin in the air." She plucks them out of the cart and puts them on the shelf.

"You have four years, Sky."

She moves me out of the way with her shoulder and pushes the cart in front of me, leaving me in aisle three. "You and I both know that isn't true."

Reluctantly I follow her and our cart of fruit, veggies, and wheat grain items. "Can we have one cheat day?" I whine like a four-year-old asking for Halloween candy.

Looking more at what's on the shelves than in front of me, I run smack dab into her back. "Shit, Sky."

She starts walking backward and I trip over my own heels to back-up. I didn't think my argument to buy the cookies was that sound, but okay...

"Go, go, go." Her voice is low and rushed.

We end up back in the temptation aisle of cookies and everything I shouldn't eat, and she ditches the cart and starts walking the other way.

"Sky?" I question.

She circles back, gives me a death stare, places her finger over her lips and waves me to follow.

Instead, I peer out into the main aisle running across the back of the store to see what has her spooked. I'm not sure what I thought I'd find, but it sure wasn't a well-built guy picking out which package of steak to buy. Other than the fact that he prefers an artery clogging meat to a leaner cut, he seems harmless.

Skylar is already at the other end of the aisle, her foot tapping, her arms crossed.

I throw my hands up in a what the fuck's the matter?

She waves frantically like there's a crack splitting in the earth between us and I have two seconds to jump before I'm swallowed up.

Walking slowly over to her, it looks like she's about to run out when I grasp her elbow to stop her. "What's the problem?"

She whips around so fast her ponytail nails me across the eyes. I blink a few times, the sting slowly fading.

Her eyes do a sweep of the immediate area and she leans in. "It's my ex-boyfriend."

I scoff. Standing taller and wishing I didn't have this damn cast on decorated with Mollys's rainbows and shit.

"Ben?" I ask.

I know his name. He screwed her up. Just like Summer did to me.

She bites down on her lip and nods.

Never in my life have I seen Skylar run from anything. Well...that's not entirely true. She's running from skiing right now if she was honest with herself.

The skiing part I understand. Her ego is bruised. She's letting herself feel down about it, when in reality, bronze is still an amazing accomplishment. But this—an ex? The ex that screwed her over by kissing her best friend at a party? We're not running away from this.

I pull on her elbow, but her feet are planted on the ground as if she's grown roots. I may be disadvantaged with one arm, but I'm stronger than her.

"You're not going to let that douche stop you from grocery shopping."

She nods, and her eyes say yes, yes, I am.

I shake my head. "No. No, you're not." I link my good hand in hers, leading us back to the cart.

I peer over the tall grocery shelf. Ben is still there. Seriously, how long does it take to pick out a steak? Skylar dodged a bullet with this one if you ask me. Coming back, I stare into her fearful eyes. Why is she scared? She should be standing up to him and saying I'm a fucking Winter Classics medalist, what do you do? Other than getting your jollies from staring at red meat for ten minutes.

"We're going to shop, and if we run into him so be it. I can handle it if you'd like." I place her hands on the cart to give them something else to do instead of clenching and unclenching at her side.

In my mind, I thought we'd have a few aisles for her to calm down or maybe he'd leave, and he'd never know we were there. Ideally, the latter would have been the best option. Sometimes in life, things don't always work like that. Nope, we step out of the aisle, rounding the corner to head into the next row and the bastard finally puts a steak in his basket and looks up.

His face transforms in three different emotions in a matter of seconds. Surprise first, along with a smile. Then a frown, probably remembering what he did to Skylar. Lastly, a soft smile that says it's nice to see her.

I'd chop him up and put him for sale in cellophane packages if I could.

CHAPTER FOUR

"Skylar?" Ben approaches and she swallows hard, plastering a smile on her pale face.

"Ben." She bites out his name, but there's still a tinge of affection in her tone that annoys me.

If I saw Summer, I'd stroll right by her without a word. Sky's different though. She might be balls to the wall protective of her friends, but when it comes to her own self, she's not as outspoken.

He places his basket down and my stomach lurches knowing exactly where his arms intend on going—around her. He holds her to him for longer than necessary—at least in my opinion when you're the prick who screwed over the woman in front of you.

Sky looks at me with widened eyes when she pulls away.

Guess we should have ditched the cart. My bad.

"You look great. Did you just get back? We watched you on television. I still have no idea how you do what you do." His face reddens and glances my way. "Sorry." He holds his hand out. "Ben Crabtree."

"Beckett Myers." I shake his hand, stopping myself from spouting out the millions of jokes running through my brain over his name.

He snaps his fingers and points to me. "You're a skier, too, right?"

"Snowboarder," I correct.

He nods and shrugs like they're the same thing. I'd like to sit him down and explain the difference, but the conversation moves quickly back and forth between the two of them with me clearly on the outside.

"The whole city is abuzz about you. Your whole family went to the Classics, right?" Ben's voice hangs on that upper octave that's annoying as shit.

Skylar's cheeks pink. Why the fuck is she blushing? This guy is no reason to blush. "Well, my parents did, then headed straight to Arizona for the rest of winter and..." she eyes my way, making Ben follow. "I'm taking care of Beckett until he's healed."

I lift my arm.

"Oh, did you get that while competing?" he asks and, in this moment, I wish I had. It'd be so much more badass if I could say I fell during a trick. Saying I slipped on ice makes me sound like an eighty-two-year-old who broke his hip.

"No," I answer curtly.

He nods, unfazed and looks back to Skylar. "We should totally catch up. What are your plans?"

Did he not catch the part where she's taking care of me? How does he know I'm not her boyfriend?

"Um, yeah, you still have my number?"

The dip wad pulls out his phone, scrolling through his contacts. His eyes light up and he shows her his screen. Doesn't say much for the guy if he's holding onto a girl's number from six years ago.

I busy myself looking at the food at the end of the aisle, picking up boxes and reading the labels. Like I'm worried about calorie content and preservatives.

"Great, Beth and I would love to have you over. Of course, she's about to pop, so, maybe we should go out where someone else can serve us."

I glance over to Skylar. Her face has lost some of its earlier luster after seeing he still had her number. She hides it well, but I know her better. Her smile teeters on creepy more than genuine.

"Great. Give me a call." Skylar's phone dings and she moves to her pocket, probably looking for any distraction she can get.

"Now you've got mine." Dear Ben leans in closer. "Let's keep that between us. You know Beth."

The corner of Skylar's lips lift for a half second before they go creepy again.

"Well, I better get going. Beth is waiting at home and had a craving for steak." He lifts his basket in the air, like either of us gives a shit about what his pregnant wife wants.

"See you around, Ben," she says.

He reaches in for another awkward hug, Skylar patting him on the back like he's the overzealous uncle everyone avoids.

"Oh, yeah, congratulations on the bronze. At least you medaled, right?"

He's shittin' me, right?

I step forward to follow the bastard, but Skylar grabs my good arm, squeezing until I stop trying to chase the asshole from the store.

"You're going to let that stupid fuck get away with that?"

I'm not even sure why I'm so angry. I'm the guy that

nothing really bothers. But this guy grated on every easy-going nerve I've got in my body. To end it like that, like bronze is a participation ribbon his damn kid will be getting in a couple of years. What has he done? Other than messing around with her best friend behind her back.

"Is that *the* Beth he was referring to?" I ask.

Skylar nods, pushing the cart down the aisle, grabbing the Oreos from the end cap. I say nothing because I want them and because if it makes her feel better her complaints afterward will be worth it.

She's silent down the next two aisles, letting me put chips, sugar cereals, and candy into the cart. No lectures, no putting them back on the shelf.

Finally, when we get to the refrigerated section and she's staring into the case of milk, she asks me, "Have you ever thought we're wasting our lives?"

She opens the door and I reach into the cooler, grabbing a gallon of milk with my good hand.

"We're living our dream."

"At the sacrifice of everything else."

"Is this because the dipshits are having a baby?" I grab a carton of cookie dough ice cream. She'll thank me later.

She shrugs. "I just...it's stupid. Forget it."

I grab the front of the cart, not letting her move forward. "Sky, you gotta let the bronze thing go. It's eating you alive."

"It's not just the bronze thing...I mean, it is...but not because I came in third. It just made me think, why am I sacrificing so much, only to be third best?"

"What are you really sacrificing? You're young. By the time your body tells you it's time to retire, you'll still be young enough to do whatever you want."

"Ben and Beth are living their lives—married, a baby on the way, probably a house. I rent my condo. I'm perpetually single. When or if I ever meet anyone, there's dating—as if I ever have the time. Then plan a wedding, I'd only have a small opening of time to get pregnant and have the baby before I have to be back on the slope." She shakes her head. "If I go back to the team, I'm looking at another four years at least before I can do any of that. Which makes me almost thirty."

"Which is young." I pause between each word, hoping she'll see my point.

"That's all if I ever meet anyone, which we both know is nearly impossible with our schedules. No male wants to take a back seat to his girlfriend's career."

She's right. I mean, I wouldn't be following a girl around the world, but I'm not your typical male. I've never had real roots.

"There's something called a beta male. Maybe we need to score you one of those."

She giggles, breaking the tension and I wrap my arm around her shoulders. "You might have to be the one with the muscles in a relationship. The one to fight off a thief in a dark alley, but hey, you can ski and have a baby."

She jabs me in the ribs with her elbow. "Let's go home, veg out with some junk food and watch movies for the rest of the night."

I take control of the cart, grabbing a container of mint chocolate chip ice cream and then we revisit the chip and cookie aisle. I know what you're thinking and you're right, I know how to let my girl deal with the fight inside of her. But that doesn't make me a beta, I'm an alpha all the way to my bones.

CHAPTER FIVE

"You pick one, I pick one." I click to the movie section of her television.

She brings a tray over filled with popcorn, candy and drinks, setting it next to my feet. I hate feeling like a lazy bum who's not helping her. I might be physically hurt, but she's emotionally injured right now, and I honestly don't know how to fix it.

Any guy would be lucky to have her, but she wasn't wrong in the store—our dreams don't make it easy to make a relationship work. And I'm sure it's even harder for female athletes because most men aren't going to quit their job to follow. Two of the couples we know best are making it work because they share the same dream. Most average Joes aren't going to throw their career aside to put her career first.

She piles her hair on top of her head, and my eyes focus on the stretch of her long neck. When did that part of her start to look so lickable?

I blink, bending forward and fisting a handful of popcorn.

"Okay, but I go first." She sits next to me and puts the bowl of popcorn in between us and hands me my drink.

"Thanks. I promise once this is off, I'm repaying you for all this nice nurse catering."

She smiles and tilts her head. "You've done it for me. What are friends for?"

"Still...thanks."

It's a hard thing for me—to feel helpless with someone. It's easier with Skylar than anyone else, but I hate relying on anyone.

I lean forward and place my drink on a coaster on the table and pass her the remote with my good hand. She immediately starts searching for a romantic comedy.

"Ugh," I groan. I had high hopes that she was in a horror film mood, but I should've guessed I'd be forced to endure some chick flick after the incident earlier today.

Why torment herself? She's depressed enough.

She scrolls and scrolls while I pull out my phone, figuring this is going to be awhile.

"Demi and Dax are coming back to the states next week," I say, checking out their Instagram picture of whatever beach they're at. Turning my phone, I show Skylar.

She glances from the television to the picture on my phone where Demi is on Dax's back with the ocean behind them. Wouldn't mind changing places with them right about now.

A smile tips her lips. "Nice."

It's then I realize that was a dick move. I just showed her how happy in love her best friend is.

"Oh!" She smacks my leg. "When Harry Met Sally."

I raise both eyebrows. "Isn't that the eighties movie where she fakes an orgasm at a restaurant table?"

She nods, her smile widening to the biggest one I've

seen all day. "I've always wanted to watch it but never have. Come on." She tilts her head, fluttering her dark eyelashes.

"Sure." I keep my phone out, scrolling through some more shit. All our teammates are off somewhere on vacation and my sorry ass is parked on a couch with poor Skylar next to me, forced to care for me. The least I can do is let her watch a movie.

"Terminator might be my choice," I warn her. She sits up straighter, pulling her legs up and crossing them on the couch. She doesn't bother to give a reaction because we both know she'll fall asleep during my movie. Though, I can't carry her to bed like normal.

The movie starts to play, and I continue messing on my phone, toying with playing a new game when she clears her throat.

"Phone away."

I roll my eyes, and I could make the argument that she'll be halfway to dreamland when Terminator starts, but after everything she's done for me, I keep my mouth shut and place my phone on the side table next to me.

By the time we're halfway through the movie, the popcorn is long gone and a handful of peanut M&M's rest in my hands. It's actually not too bad for a chick flick. I've laughed more than usual. The only thing, and it's a big thing for me, is that it's about friends who obviously like one another. Which only brings all that shit Dax and Grady keep throwing my way to mind.

I glance over at Sky—she's laughing and smiling and that warms my heart more than it should. My speech to Dax when he messed up with Demi was heartfelt because it's what I would do if I was a different person. I'd smash my lips to hers until we both saw stars. I'm not blind to the amazing woman she is. I hate to use the whole 'it's you not me,' but it's the truth.

Everyone thinks I'm all laidback and full of forgiveness, but I come with baggage. Garbage bags full of trash and if we ever tiptoed over that line, I'd lose her in the end. So, I'll let you in on a little secret, I want Skylar Walsh, but the hell if I'll ever make a move because I'd rather have her in my life as a friend than not in my life at all.

"Sorry." She knocks me in the shoulder and swings back her way. "Bored, huh?"

I'm not sure how long I was off in la-la land—thank God she didn't force me to watch that movie—but the television is paused, and all her attention is on me.

"No, it's a pretty funny movie."

She pretends like she's scrutinizing my answer, but quickly presses play and the movie begins again. Just like that, we're back to two friends enjoying the movie and I try to push back my attraction to her. It's only surfacing because of all the husband and baby talk today in the grocery store. I'm confident my unresolved feelings will pass, they always do.

The movie ends and I'm back in control of myself once again. I've taken the blanket from our laps and given it to her. When I got up to take a piss, I sat far enough away when I returned that her perfume wasn't intoxicating me. And when I looked in her direction, I looked over her shoulder and didn't make direct eye contact. All of that worked and now I'm back to cool, calm and collected.

"Do you ever think about dating?" Skylar asks me out of nowhere.

A light sheen of sweat coats my forehead. So much for cool. "No."

She turns her body in my direction, but I don't engage.

"Beck." She throws an M&M at me. "I never see you with a girl."

Because none of the girls are you.

I shrug. "We've been over this. I'm not that into monogamy."

She huffs. "Have there been girls?"

Why is she asking this? We keep our private affairs, private. How do you think I've been able to keep my self respect by not going all alpha on guys sniffing around her?

"Do I need to go over our friendship pact again?" I ask with some humor.

About a month after Skylar and I started spending so much time together, we made an agreement. No talking about the opposite sex. No engaging in overly affectionate behavior. Who knows where that stupid drunk list went.

"You probably can't remember three things from that stupid list. We were both half conked from a bottle of tequila."

"It's been four years and we're closer than ever, so we must be doing something right."

She smiles and leans her head against my shoulder. "I'm not sure what I would do without you."

Me either.

"Good thing I'm not attracted to you then."

She balks, sits up straight and stares down at me. I'm not sure if she wants to cry or punch me in the balls.

"Hey, you're beautiful, but I just don't see you like that," I lie.

She nods, a soft smile forming on her lips.

Don't be pissed off at me, I have to say those things once in awhile just to make sure she knows what side of the line we need to stay on.

"Are blondes your type?"

Fuck, she's in her needy stage where she's depressed and she wants reconfirmation that she's a hot piece of ass guys watch as she walks by.

I shrug. "You know you're gorgeous, Sky."

"Then how come I don't have anyone? You don't find me attractive..."

She continues but I drown her out before I grind my dick into her center to show her exactly how attracted I am to her.

"I'm sure you don't see me for the stud I am either," I joke.

I wiggle to the edge of the couch and stand, needing an out of this conversation.

"No, you're hot. I can acknowledge it."

"But?" I ask and disappear into the kitchen. I need a beer.

"But nothing. I admire you at times." She follows me.

I hold the beer out in her direction and she twists off the cap for me, tossing it into the garbage. "I admire you too, but—"

She holds up her hand. "I know, Beck, I'm not your type." Rounding the counter, she disappears out of the kitchen. "I'm heading to bed."

Fuck me. Damn that shithead Ben from the grocery store. This is when being friends with a woman is so much harder than with a guy.

"Sky." I follow her down the hall and up the stairs. "You need..." I swallow down the bile burning my throat.

She turns around when she reaches her childhood bedroom door. The same room that has pictures of Ben on her corkboard from some dance way back when. The room that holds all her memories of a happy childhood filled with fun, laughter and love. Doesn't she realize, she has so much?

"What?"

"You need a date."

Did that really just come out of my mouth?

"A date?"

I grab her hand and take her into my room, which is really her brother's childhood room, and sit her down on the bed.

"Yeah, give me your phone."

She digs it out of her pocket and places it in my palm.

I search the app store and select a dating app.

"GeekMatch?"

"Yep."

"What about the more traditional ones?" she asks, leaning over to look at my phone. Her hair tickles my neck, and the scent of her perfume makes my dick twitch in my pants.

"You need a beta, remember?"

"Hmm."

I go through her selfies and select one that doesn't show how truly gorgeous she is. It's hard to find one though because Skylar doesn't have any bad pictures.

"I'm not sure about this, Beck."

I fill out her form for her while she remains silent. Once I'm done, I hand it back over to her and she stares at the screen for a long time.

Our thighs are pressed against one another and I'm fairly sure the electricity running through my body is buzzing through hers, but her gaze is still glued to her phone.

"Okay," she says, still sounding reluctant.

"Perfect. Now, Terminator."

She smiles and her lips brush my cheek. "Sorry, for being so needy."

"It's the hazard of having girl friends, I suppose."

"Friends?"

"Friend," I clarify, standing up before my hands and lips listen to the instructions from my dick.

"You'll help me pick someone out?" she asks.

"Of course."

She walks out of my room, her gaze glued to her phone. I follow with my gaze glued to her ass. I know I'm playing with fire, but at least with GeekMatch, I can guarantee the guy will treat her right.

CHAPTER SIX

Two nights later, the real test of my steadfastness happens.

Skylar's heels click on her parents' linoleum floor. I'm standing in the living room and I force my gaze to stay locked on the television, my breath catching in my throat. After my internal pep talk for the past half hour, I should have this.

"Zip me?" She turns her back to me and I swallow down the dry lump in my throat.

The opening of her dress lands right at her panty line, showcasing her pink silk undies with lace along the top. I step back just to make sure my now bulging dick doesn't end up poking her in the back.

My shaking fingers grab a hold of the zipper and I slowly pull it up along her olive colored skin until it lands mid back.

"There you go." The tremble in my voice matches my heart rate.

"Thanks." She twirls around like a school girl getting

ready for a dance. "What do you think?" The smile slowly fading from her lips. "What?"

"Nothing. You look great."

She does. I've seen Skylar at her worst. Bedridden with the flu and smelling of puke. Three days into no sleep with a dry red nose from a head cold. Hungover with stringy hair and bad breath. Then there's been the sponsor galas with her hair pinned up and red-colored lips. Tonight, she's got her girl next door look perfected. Not too much makeup, a light gloss along her plump lips and a dress that shows her assets but isn't inviting any takers.

"Do I look fuckable?"

I choke on the saliva in my throat. "What?" I ask when I'm done coughing. "I mean, you're not..."

She pushes me lightly in the shoulder and I lose my footing. "You know me better than that."

Jesus.

"That doesn't mean I don't want to look the part though."

"Well, then mission accomplished, but don't make me give him the dad speech."

She giggles. A sound I love hearing but it's not as sweet knowing it's for another guy who's going to be here any second.

"Drink to make the nerves disappear?" I'm already on my way to the liquor cabinet to grab the hardest shit Skylar's dad has on hand. Sadly, he seems to be a mixed drinker which means his choice of scotch isn't one malt.

"Sure. I'm not even sure why I'm nervous. It's not like I haven't dated before." She follows me, her heels a constant reminder that she's looking amazing for someone else.

"When was the last time you were out on a date?" I ask,

pulling two glasses out from her dad's makeshift bar in the dining room.

"Now that I think about it...other than Sam—"

"Sam? Sam on the team Sam?"

She accepts the glass and tentatively sips. "Yeah, we went out a few times in New Zealand during training this past summer."

Traitor.

"I didn't know."

She waves her hand at me. "It was nothing."

He's still a fucking traitor.

The door opens and the sound of little footsteps racing through the hall echo out and seconds later Molly and Caiden are heading right for Skylar.

She holds up her hands and they skid to a stop, freezing in place with wide eyes. Molly approaches slowly, and Caiden climbs into the chair at the bar.

"Aunt Skylar, you look pretty." Molly slides right up to the chair on the other side of Caiden.

"What will you two troublemakers be having tonight?" I ask.

Molly pretends to think while Caiden throws his hand on the bar. "A Miller."

Skylar laughs, but Zoe and Vin round the corner of the room as Zoe shoots Vin a what the fuck look.

He holds his hands up in the air ready to defend himself when his gaze finds me and his arm extends. "Beckett, I hear you gave Molly quite the show."

Zoe slaps him in the stomach and he pretends her tiny slap could hurt him. The man is six three, two fifty at least.

"Nice try," I say.

Zoe doesn't do any more scolding to her husband

though because her eyes light up and she smiles when she spots Skylar. Her gaze shifts to me and her smile dims.

"Gotta hot date?" she asks.

"Yeah," Skylar says and nods her head toward the kitchen and the two sisters disappear.

"Since the little guy is having a Miller, what will the lady have?" I ask Molly.

"Kiddie Cocktail," she answers, straightening her back and acting like she asked for tea and crumpets.

"That's an order I can handle." I toss a glass in the air and catch it, two sets of little eyes on me the entire time.

Vin walks up and pats me on the back, hard. I cough and manage to keep the Sprite pouring into the glass. "I'm one-armed here."

"You're going to have a lot of lessons to learn when you and Sky have kids. The first one being always lock the bedroom and the bathroom doors." He winks and walks around to take the third seat at the bar while I grab a Miller for him. Skylar's parents must be the party house for fifty-somethings because the place is stocked.

"You've got a few things wrong there," I say.

He raises an eyebrow.

"Marriage and kids are not for me."

"Not for you?" he questions.

I shrug.

Vin and I are usually drinking buddies when we see each other. We talk sports with Skylar's brother, Mike, shoot the shit about politics and anything other than our philosophies on life.

Setting down a pair of small napkins with a W embossed on them, I place the two kiddie cocktails down and the kids grin at each other.

"Why not?" Vin asks.

What I'm about to say will sound awful, but Vin's biggest dream through high school was probably to get laid. Not that I wasn't all for that, too, but we grew up differently and it shaped our views of the world. When he graduated he went to work with his dad. He's always had a safety net.

I shrug. Is it really his business? No.

"Marrying Zoe and having these two rug rats was the best thing that ever happened to me." He tousles each one of his kid's heads and they give him an adoring smile. They love their dad and that's great—for him.

"They're great kids and Zoe's okay."

He laughs understanding the push/pull relationship I have with his wife.

"So is Sky…"

I nod, pouring myself another glass of scotch. "No denying that."

"Then why are you letting her go out on a date?" He guzzles some of his beer, leaning back into his chair.

"Because Skylar wants what you guys have."

"She said that?" His forehead wrinkles.

"I'm sure she'd rather not have her husband take her son to a bar so that he's ordering Millers as a drink, but in so many words."

He shakes his head then downs his beer. "Are all snowboarders like you?"

Vin's met Grady and Dax and a few of the other snowboarders when the family came to visit Sky in Utah.

"How's that?" I rest my ass against the back counter of the bar, crossing my ankles.

"Selfish."

Little does he know, I'm doing the least selfish thing I can tonight. I'm watching the woman I want under me go out with another man. Hell, I'm encouraging it.

"You think I'm selfish?"

He nods. The kids slide out of their chairs and run off to the playroom.

Vin leans forward, his muscular forearms from his labor-intensive job flexing under his weight. "You won't put your own shit aside for a woman."

He just doesn't understand.

"That's not it."

"Sure, it is." He stands, downing the rest of his beer and placing the empty on the bar top.

"It's not."

He nods, heading toward the kitchen but the girls beat him to it.

"Miss me?" Zoe asks, placing her arms around her husband's shoulders.

He dips her and kisses her making for an uncomfortable silence for the two of us not in the exchange. Skylar stares on with envy in her eyes, while annoyance wraps around me like a tight leash. When the doorbell rings Vin pops Zoe back up, leaving her breathless.

"Maybe Beck should answer. Freak the poor guy out a little." Zoe giggles, leaning into her husband's strong arms.

Yeah, thanks for that Zoe.

"I doubt I'll scare him with one usable arm." I step out from behind the bar because the masochistic part of me needs to get a look at this guy.

"Sky." Vin dislodges himself from his wife, kissing Skylar on the cheek. "You look gorgeous, he's one lucky guy." He separates from her and shoots me an evil stare.

What the hell did I do to these people?

I say nothing because now that the moment is here, I'm thinking this was a shit brain idea. Opening the door, the guy stands there, sweat on his forehead, the flowers in his hand shaking more than my legs after a long day of riding.

"Hey," I say.

"Hi." He draws back looking at the address plaque beside the door. "Is Skylar here?" he asks, his voice shaking more than his hands.

Poor schmuck. When was the last time he was on a date?

"She is. Who are you?"

"I'm Tad."

"Tad?" *What kind of fucking name is that?*

"Yes, I'm her date for tonight."

"Ohhh...she mentioned something about that." I usher him in with my hand. "Come in. Drink while you wait?"

As he stands in Skylar's parents' foyer, I examine my competition. I guess he's not really my competition since I'm not playing the game, but whatever.

"What do you do?" I ask.

He uses his free hand to push it through his short red hair, his cheeks so red I fear he's having an allergic reaction.

"Hi, Tad." Skylar rounds the corner.

I keep my eyes on her date. No need to see her energetic smile.

Molly and Caiden run in, sliding to a stop on their socks.

Tad's eyes widen.

"Honey, did you not tell him about the kids?"

Skylar narrows her eyes at me.

"Sorry, Tad, we were just leaving. It's my weekend and all." I grab their coats off the hooks near the door with my good hand.

"Oh, your profile didn't say—"

"Forget him. This is my friend Beckett." Skylar grabs

her own coat from the hook and the nice guy Tad is, helps her get it on. What a gentleman.

"Are you?" He tilts his head. "I recognize you from the Winter Classics, right?"

"Yeah," I answer and then he looks at Skylar.

"And you?"

She nods.

"I've seen you guys on commercials!" His face lights up with excitement. "Whoa, my mom is going to be so impressed I'm going out with a Winter Classics athlete." His hand moves to his pocket but then he stops. Good move, Tad.

"We should probably go." Skylar rolls up and down on her heels.

"Yeah, oh, um." He turns back to me, holding his hand out. "Could I just get one picture? My mom..."

"Sure. You don't mind, right, Sky?"

"Not at all," she says between clenched teeth.

"Oh here." Zoe saunters in, holding her hand out for his phone and the flowers. "I'll take one of all three you."

Tad looks around the room.

"Sister." Zoe points to herself. "Brother-in-law." She points to Vin and he gives a little wave. "Niece and nephew." The two kids look up and smile.

"But I thought..." Tad wiggles his finger between Molly and Caiden and then points to me and back to the kids.

"I was kidding."

"Oh." His head falls back like I just told the funniest joke he's heard all year. When we went on GeekMatch I thought that would entail a date with someone who was highly intelligent. I think we got scammed.

Skylar blows out a breath and Tad holds the phone out to Zoe.

"Now, all of you get nice and close."

Vin steps forward and takes Molly and Caiden's coats from my good hand. Tad gets in the middle, I have to switch spots with Skylar so that my bad arm is on the outside. We all smile big and a flash blinds us.

"Looks good." Zoe hands it back and Tad's like a teenager checking it out before we all move in case we need to take another one.

"Perfect, my mom—"

"Is going to love it," all three of us say in unison.

Skylar opens the door, and has one foot outside before Tad has even processed it's time to start his date. Totally clueless and I have to admit that a part of me is not disappointed about it. No way this guy is going to try to get in Sky's pants tonight.

"Have fun you two!" Zoe calls out the door like I'm assuming Tad's mom might do. Hell, she might be in the car waiting to drive them to the restaurant.

The door shuts and Zoe's fun demeanor turns cold and icy in an instant. "Kids get your coats from your dad and put on your shoes, Daddy is taking us out."

"But I wanted to have game night. Uncle Beckett will play," Molly whines.

"I'm totally game for Monopoly, Life. Pick your poison, kid." I wink.

"No, Uncle Beckett likes to be alone. Alone and unattached."

"Zoe," I sigh.

She puts her hand up in the air. "Have a great night, Beckett."

The kids get ready, Vin shooting me a 'I'm sorry' expression. After hugs from the kids, Zoe peeks her head in the doorway one more time. "Don't think about her with Tad too much. She's had a dry spell so I'm fairly sure it won't take much."

Slam.

Mission accomplished, Zoe. Now *all* I can think about is that maybe I was wrong about that doofus Tad. What if he has what it takes to seduce Skylar...where would that leave me?

CHAPTER SEVEN

A lot of shit has been a pain in the ass since I broke my arm, but the worst is typing on my phone. My laptop collects dust in the corner and I lean my back on the headboard, scrolling through Instagram again.

I like my alone time, but tonight, I'm bored as fuck because of this damn injury. Usually I'd be in Park City, hanging out at my go-to bars or messing around on my board.

Clicking on my new notifications, my stomach drops when I see the name of the person who just started following me. Too curious for my own good, I click on her profile.

Summer Gorges. Although she's crossed my mind on occasion, usually as a reminder not to make the same mistake twice, I haven't seen her in a long time.

I click on her selfie profile pic. Her hair is still a light shade of purple and she has a grim look on her face like it would kill her to smile. She has an amazing smile, but hell if she'll let anyone in. She's still closed off from the world. I can't say I blame her, I might have been abandoned, but

Summer, she was the cases people talk about. Abused, neglected and finally abandoned at that pre-teen age when kids have no self-confidence. For a moment in time, she let me peek into that small world of hers.

Sadness seeps in seeing it's mostly her and her friends in all her pictures. Drinking and partying. Looks like she works as a barista in Coronado. She didn't get that far from our hometown then.

My thumb hovers over the message button. She followed me, so is that what she expects? She made the first move. Is she waiting to see if I'll make the next one?

A soft knock lands on my door and I press the home button, tucking my phone under my leg.

"Come in," I say.

Skylar peeks her head into the room. "You're still up?"

"Well, you knocked on my door."

She opens the door all the way up, dropping the heels hanging from her fingers outside the door. Comfortable as always, she cozies up on the bed with me, careful not to flash me.

"How was your date with Tad?"

She shrugs. "A little too enamored over the fact I'm a professional skier."

Hazard of the job. Hell, girls have slept with me just to say they did. Dax has been plastered all over social media sleeping in bed with the girl's face in the picture, pointing to him. It's hard to find someone who wants you for you alone.

"Sorry, but hey, you probably made his mom's day."

She leans into me, ready to knock me in the shoulder with hers, but I wrap my good arm around her shoulders and keep her next to me. The scent of vanilla from her shampoo permeates the air around us, arousing me. As much as I hate to admit it, I missed her tonight, so much I need to get better and back to Park City ASAP. Because I cannot rely on Skylar any more than I already do. Nothing good can come of it.

"After dinner, he FaceTimed his mom." She cringes. "She was sweet though."

"Uh-huh." I roll my eyes.

"At least he treats his mom nice."

"True." I pause for a moment before I ask my next question. "Did you kiss him goodnight?"

It's none of my business and goes against the rules we put into effect years ago.

"On the cheek."

Good girl.

"Here." I hold my palm out for her phone.

She shakes her head. "I think I'll pick the next one on my own."

I can't say that I blame her. Tad was my choice and he turned out to be a mama's boy.

We sit in silence, the sound of the movie I was half watching filling the empty space created by our silence.

"Sky?"

She turns to me, crossing her ankles and I can't help but look at the smooth skin of her legs.

"Is this all because you got bronze?"

"What?" Does she really not realize how much she's changed since we returned? How she's turned away from the dreams we once shared and is now heading in a completely different direction.

"The whole wanting a family and grad school thing. You thinking you're missing out on something."

"No. I mean I'm pissed about getting bronze, but I'm still happy I medaled. I can't in good faith complain, but I've been questioning what's next for me for a while. Sooner or later it's going to end, and I don't want to be the old veteran still trying to keep up. The one people whisper about behind their back."

If she'd gotten silver or gold, she wouldn't be saying this. The fact that the gold and silver medalists were far younger than her doesn't help.

"You're an amazing skier," I say with conviction.

"I know."

"Look who's cocky." I chuckle.

She laughs and throws her legs over the side of the bed to leave.

"You don't want the other stuff, so you wouldn't understand. Skiing is only a chapter in my life, Beck, not the whole book, and I'm thinking my next chapter should be starting soon."

She walks toward the door and I deny the urge inside willing me to ask her to stay. "I'm here for you, whatever you decide," I say instead.

She smiles, the light from the hallway pouring over her body. "I guess it was bound to happen one day, right?"

I tilt my head. "What?"

"Us going in different directions."

My chest hurts, and I swear I hear the crack in my heart like it's a gif that people send one another.

She doesn't wait for me to answer, instead shutting my door, leaving me in the dark with just the glow of the television.

I examine my arm in the sling. I need to get healed and get the hell out of Dodge. I've clearly overstayed my welcome—even if I'm the only one who knows it.

CHAPTER EIGHT

Skylar breezes into her former high school, a friendly smile on her face as she greets the receptionist and office staff.

"Oh, Skylar Walsh, you look even more beautiful than on television." The elderly lady with permed hair says.

"Everyone knows TV adds ten pounds." Another woman approaches, taking Skylar into her arms. There should be a handout for age-appropriate clothes. This lady needs more layers.

"And who's this?" The first lady peeks over Skylar's shoulder.

Skylar backs up a step, placing her hand on my shoulder. "This is my friend Beckett Myers. He competed in the Classics in snowboarding."

The skimpy clothed lady narrows her eyes like she's trying to place me. Should I tick off the commercials I've done or mention the press promo ads? For two weeks every four years, even I'm surprised how much my face shows up on national television. Then it's a blackout until three months before the next Classics. Unless you're my buddy, Grady Kale. That guy scored one hell of an agent.

"Oh, I remember you. My grandson said you should have won," the elderly lady says.

I shrug like I could care less. I'm not ungrateful for my silver, but yeah, the judges kind of screwed me in my opinion. "Tell him hi and thanks for being a fan."

"You should speak, too. I mean how many times do we have two Classic medalists in our small little school."

"Nah, this is Skylar's thing." I wave them off.

This school is nothing like the campuses where I grew up. It's all enclosed. Our lockers were outside, and we could sneak off easily. Yeah, I wasn't an A student.

A bell rings and the older lady scurries behind her desk, staring into a camera and then clicks a button. "Your cousin is here," she says to Skylar.

"Chelsea?" I ask, looking over at Sky. "You didn't tell me."

"You wouldn't have come." She shrugs.

I nod. She's got a point. There's nothing wrong with Chelsea if you appreciate a girl with no filter. Think Dax with a set of tits and more attitude.

"Oh, what's not to love about Chelsea?" The woman who might be giving the freshman boys their wet dream material scoots to the door, never really picking up her high heels.

Chelsea walks in, her blonde hair like a makeshift bird's nest from the Chicago wind. She unzips her coat and Skylar starts laughing while I shake my head. Skiers rule snowboarders drool is printed on her t-shirt.

"That would hold more weight if you skied, Chelsea," I say.

She gives the lady a hug, they exchange a few words and then she pulls me into her clutches.

"Oh, Beckett, I always love razzing you." She kisses my cheek and then pushes me back.

"Hello? Arm?" I hold up it up.

"You haven't been freed of that thing yet?" She moves on to Skylar, the two having a shared whisper conversation. I faintly hear something about balls and I step back.

"Marge," Chelsea coos, heading behind the desk and pulling the older lady to her. "I miss this place."

Chelsea and Skylar are cousins. Same age, so you can imagine how fun it is when the three of us are together. Usually they gossip about people I've never met in my fucking life. Good times.

"What are you up to these days?" the other woman asks.

My gaze flicks to the big clock wondering when this shindig gets started.

"Yeah, Chels, have you found a job yet?" I ask, twisting the screwdriver she brought with her when she chose to wear that shirt.

Her head swivels in my direction, a smug smile in place and then she looks back to Marge. "I did. I'm going to be head of marketing and PR for a new non-profit."

"Chels, that's great!" Skylar hugs her from behind, Chelsea patting her cousin's hand.

She went the college route and has ping-ponged through as many jobs as tricks I've landed safely. In other words, a shit ton.

"The owner is super awesome. Female."

They all say 'oh,' like that's some big thing. Haven't women been pushing that glass ceiling for a while now? I don't see how that's a surprise.

"It's just starting out, so I can really prove myself. I'm so excited."

"Did you start already?" Skylar asks.

"Tomorrow." She crosses both her fingers in the air.

Skylar hugs her one more time. "I'm so proud of you."

"Yeah, you're employed." I do a little cheer with my good arm and Chelsea narrows her eyes at me.

"How's the arm, Beckett? Still need Skylar to nurse you back to health?" She raises her voice an octave like she's speaking to a baby.

"Oh, great, you're here! The students are getting restless. Come on." A dark-haired woman peeks into the room.

"Sorry." Skylar shoots me a tight smile and I give her a thumbs-up.

We all file out of the office, the two ladies wishing Skylar luck and gushing about Chelsea's new job. Did I miss the part where she says she cured cancer?

Walking down Skylar's high school hallways on the way to the gym, memories of Summer wash over me. How young I was. I wasn't as jaded yet and still believed that what I'd experienced in my youth didn't have any repercussions. My experience with Summer convinced me otherwise.

The dark-haired lady stops us right before we're going to enter the gym doors. Chelsea is giving Skylar a pep talk and I lean against the wall. The woman who I think at some point on our walk over here said her name was Gwen, has her attention poised on whoever is talking in the gym.

"Winter Classics medalist, Skylar Walsh!" The man on the microphone announces and clapping rings out from the large room.

She walks across the gym floor to join the man at the microphone while Chelsea and I are guided to two open spots in the front row. Sky's shaky hand lands on the microphone and she swallows, so loud you can catch the faint sound over the speakers.

"She's fucking hot," some kid a few rows back says.

"She went to school here?" another adds.

"Man, what happened? The selection has gone to shit since she was here," the first kid chimes in.

Chelsea shakes her head and glances at me. I'm surprised she's yet to say anything. Silence isn't her style.

"Hey." A tap hits my shoulder and I look behind me, finding a blond kid with blue eyes, wearing a letterman jacket. Probably the school jock. There's some pin thing on his letter. "She available?"

Chelsea laughs. "In your wet dreams."

The kid narrows his eyes and I can tell he's about to unleash some of his 'I run this school venom' on her.

"Sorry, she's not," I answer nicely.

"Are you her boyfriend?" the other one asks.

"In *his* wet dream," Chelsea adds, and the kid opens his mouth but shuts it quickly.

He's probably wondering about Chelsea now. She's not hard on the eyes either.

"Actually." She taps her lips. "He could be if we traveled back in time to before he became a blind douchebag."

The boys slide closer to her, effectively knocking a girl off the bench. She pushes up her glasses, sits back down and hits the guy closest to the end with her hip. Way to fight back. There's the type of girl I should've dated in high school.

"First Zoe and now you?"

She lifts one shoulder. "Our family is close. We talk. Have your ears been burning?"

Skylar clears her throat over the mic. "My good friend,

Beckett Myers is here, too. He's a snowboarder." She waves me up.

"He's totally fucking her," the kid with the letterman jacket says.

Chelsea turns around. "No, he isn't."

Skylar's in the middle of the gym floor, waving me up because I'm fairly sure she's uncomfortable being up there by herself. I got the two horniest boys behind me hell-bent on making this a horrible experience for me. Both options suck.

"Shut. It," I grind out through my clenched jaw.

Chelsea laughs in my face and turns back to the boys. "They're friends," she says using quotations around friends.

"No such thing." The one kid gives his opinion, which no one asked for.

"That's what I said." Chelsea slaps me on the back. "Your *friend* is requesting your assistance."

I hunch over and stand, heading to the middle of the stage.

The man who I'm guessing is the principal stands and shakes my hand. "Wish I'd known we would have had both of you."

"Nah, this is Sky's thing, not mine."

"Surely your high school would like you to talk."

"Yeah, probably not." I nod and turn my focus to Skylar.

I can read her like the slopes. Easy to find my line, which path will get me there the fastest. But today she's throwing me for a loop. Skylar doesn't get scared, she doesn't get intimidated, not by this sort of thing.

She offers me the microphone and I figure to make the whole situation better, I'll take it with the hopes she'll collect herself enough to come back. Truthfully, I'll just brag about her, since she is my favorite subject.

"Hey, everyone. I'm Beckett." My eyes scan the crowd of kids until it lands on the tall figure in the corner by the doors. You have to be shitting me. This guy is fucking everywhere and it's like he's got a noose around my girl's neck.

It's not hard to figure out that Ben is a physical education teacher from his shorts, t-shirt and a damn whistle around his neck. His eyes are intent on Skylar, so I step to the side, blocking his view of her. He doesn't deserve it anyway.

CHAPTER NINE

"What is the deal with this Ben fucker?" I glance over to Skylar in the driver's seat of her mom's minivan.

Please explain why people who don't have small children have minivans? Sure, it's stocked with two car seats, no double Molly and Caiden's, but an SUV or a sedan would do Skylar's parents just fine. Even if I did have kids, I sure as shit wouldn't own a loser cruiser.

She shrugs, biting down on her bottom lip.

"Come on, Sky, you know you can tell me."

Her hands are at ten and two, her eyes fixated on the road ahead like we're driving through a blizzard.

"Nothing."

I turn in my seat. "It's not nothing. Come on. You lose all that feistiness I love so much when he's around. So, the guy broke your heart...it was a million years ago."

"He slept with my best friend."

"Again, a million years ago."

Her foot presses harder on the accelerator and I place

my palm on the roof as she takes a turn so fast I'm surprised we're not on two wheels.

"It's stupid. I need to get out of this town. How can Chicago feel so damn small?"

The car jerks to a stop before we rear end the SUV in front of us.

"I think I should drive," I say.

"Didn't Chelsea know he worked there? Why didn't she give me a heads up? No, 'surprise.'" Both her hands raise up in the air, her fingers spreading. "Let's fuck with Skylar some more."

"I think you should follow that sign to the hospital. Ask for the psych ward." I point to the blue sign on my right that we just flew past. "Or hell, let me drive one handed." My arm straightens, my palm locking to the roof as she makes another sharp turn.

I don't even know if we're five minutes or twenty minutes from home. All the streets look the same in this city.

"Skylar!" I yell right before we hit a patch of snow and ice and skid along the road and hit the parked car on our right.

"Oh, my God. Oh, my God!" Panic flashes in her eyes, her hand on my thigh. "Your arm. Tell me I didn't hurt you anymore!"

I'm a little dazed, but the airbags didn't deploy so the hit couldn't have been as bad as I anticipated it would be.

"I'm good."

She gets out, cars around us slowing down, some stopping to see what happened. A police car siren rings out almost immediately and I guess that's what you get when you're in a city. If this were Park City, I'd be shooting the shit with the person I hit for hours while we waited for the cops.

A police cruiser pulls in behind Skylar's parents' mini-van, the lights reflecting on the glass of the store windows past the sidewalk where a few bystanders linger around.

Skylar's in and out of the van, distraught and searching for the paperwork she's going to need.

"I can't believe I hit a car." She leans in and reaches toward the glovebox. I unbuckle myself, figuring as hard as it will be, I gotta get out to help.

"Hold on there, Sir." One of the police officers stands behind Skylar, directing me with his open palm.

Skylar stops, widens her eyes at me and then swivels around slowly to face the officer, who if you ask me is way too close to her ass. She draws back.

See? I told you he was too close.

"Ma'am, you need to stay in the van," the officer says.

Skylar waves him off. "I'm fine."

"Ma'am, stay in the vehicle."

"Oh please, I am not a ma'am." She relents climbing back into the driver's seat, her hands landing on her thighs. "I'm twenty-five."

A slow smirk appears on the cop's lips but he's quick to straighten it out. "Mind telling me what happened here." He pulls out his pad and pen from his front shirt pocket.

Knock, knock.

I jump, my eyes looking out the window beside me at the partner of the cop currently questioning Skylar. My guy doesn't look as nice, either that or he wishes I looked more like Skylar.

Twisting my body, I reach over to open the window. This one is not so quick to tell me to stay in place.

"Your arm?"

"Already like this." I stare down at the sling. "Obviously."

"Obviously." He hooks his thumbs on his belt and leans back.

Meanwhile to my left, Skylar's flirtatious laugh mixes with the cop's chuckle.

"How are you feeling? Well enough to sit tight for a second?" the police officer asks. "I don't want to take any chances with that arm. The paramedics will be here soon."

"No worries. I'm good."

Then the man who owns the car Skylar hit comes over ranting and raving about the damage. The officer who was just at my window places his hand in the air to stop the man from going over to Skylar.

The only good thing about this situation is, by making an appearance, Skylar and Mr. Mount Me police officer have to cut short their flirting to deal with the irate man.

Mount Me directs Skylar to leave the vehicle and head toward the back of the van and I attempt to swivel in my seat to see what's happening, but damn it, they're right at the corner. My gaze shifts back to the No Personality cop who's reassuring the frantic man that the situation is under control and he's sure we have insurance. Hello, we're in a minivan. This car screams responsibility.

Skylar comes over, opens the driver's side door and opens the glove compartment so it hits my knees.

"Beck, I think he's going to ask me for my phone number," she whispers, the worry that lined all the features of her face now taken over by a full-wattage smile.

"Because you hit another car? Two words—police report."

She giggles in a way that I've never heard before. I look up to find Mount Me outside the car, enjoying his view of her ass. Isn't there some law or something against him doing that?

She slaps my knee in a friendly 'you're joking' when in reality, I'm thinking I better not be joking. I'll be half-tempted to tattle on him to his chief. That has to be against the rules—to hit on someone you're going to ticket.

Turning back around, she hands over her license and I'm assuming what is her parents' insurance card.

"Are you the skier Skylar Walsh?" Mount Me asks. Great, might as well pull out the cell phones right now for them to exchange numbers.

I roll my eyes. Skylar twirls a strand of her hair, tilting her head softly to the side. The embarrassed innocent schoolgirl look? I thought Sky was better than that.

"Yeah." Her voice is soft and meek instead of the ferocious lioness she actually is.

"That's crazy. I mean, you were all over the news. A local skier in the Classics." He peeks his head into the car at me, drawing his eyebrows together like he's not impressed.

Well, I'm not either buddy. Do your job so I can get the fuck out of this mommy missile and back to the couch, taking the girl you're admiring with me.

"I'm back home for awhile."

"How long is awhile?" His voice drops an octave.

God, am I this ridiculous when I flirt with someone? I hope not. He's pathetic. Not to mention he has a job to do. You don't see me stopping in the middle of my run to hit on a girl standing on the fence line.

"A few weeks." She shrugs.

Usually this is the point where she signals to me to get her out of this and tells everyone that she's taking care of me. Not this time. Not even a glance over her shoulder.

I slide my butt up to the edge of the seat, one good thing about a minivan is all the open space.

More lights stop behind the van. I turn my head to look. An ambulance. Fucking hell.

The side door of the minivan opens and who should appear on the other side, but none other than Officer No Personality.

"Sir, I asked you to stay put."

"And I told you I'm fine."

Skylar's laugh slices my chest like a knife as it floats across the van.

The paramedics run over, one of the guys fist bumping the other. I guess all must know one another here.

"Just a fender bender, Luca. The guy says he's good," the cop says to the one paramedic.

"I am good. I already broke my arm."

"Let's just have a look. What harm can it do?" Luca kneels down to look at me. I realize that he bears an odd resemblance to Officer No Personality, but from the smile on his face, even if they are related they don't share personalities.

"How'd you break it?" Luca, whose patch on his uniform reads Bianco, says.

"I slipped on ice trying to save that one." I thumb in the direction of Skylar who I think might have forgotten I was even here.

"No cool story, huh?" he laughs, peeking under the sling gently. I think the two of us must be similar. If I could tell everyone I broke my arm because I fell from forty feet in the air, it'd be way cooler.

"Nothing to impress anyone," I say.

Luca glances through the minivan to Skylar. "If you've got her chaperoning you I wouldn't say that."

Does he not see her twirling her hair for Officer Mount Me?

"She's a friend. I helped her through a broken leg two years ago. She was guilted into helping me."

He chuckles, standing up and jotting something down on his notepad. "What the hell do you two do that you're breaking bones so often?"

I could lie, but what's the point. Our pseudo-celebrity status might get Sky out of a ticket if I tell the truth. "She's a skier and I snowboard."

"No shit? Like X Games or you mean you just head to Wisconsin?"

I laugh. "We just got back from the Winter Classics."

"Impressive." He glances back to the officer and their gazes both shift to Skylar. "You're telling me that she's a Classics skier?" They seem to be looking at her with admiration.

"Yep."

"Man, I feel like I gotta check you out more. I've never met an athlete like you before, though I was on the set of a television show last year."

"Don't bring that shit up again," Officer NP says. "It was for like a second."

Paramedic Good Time stands up. "More than your sorry ass got, Cristian."

So, Officer NP has a name.

"Well, at least I'm Mom's favorite," Cristian says.

Luca slaps him in the chest and my eyes zoom in on the matching name patch. Bianco.

Brothers.

"You're brothers?" I ask.

Luca's lips tip into a smirk. "What gave it away? Our matching mugs or the nameplates?"

He doesn't wait for me to answer, instead, he looks at his brother. "I'm her baby."

"Yeah, the oops baby," Officer Bianco smiles and shows some teeth.

"You broke her heart when you moved out." Luca tsks, but I can tell he's teasing.

"She'd have us wait until we're married and move in with our wives."

Paramedic looks over to me. "Italian Mama." Like that should say it all.

My only come back is "No Mama."

"Mind if we grab a picture?" Luca says. "You know to impress the chicks that I meet at the bar tonight."

I can't help but laugh at this guy. How different can two brothers be?

The other paramedic takes a picture of me and the cool brother who insisted on getting my number so that he can 'check-up' on me. I think it's really so he can flash it to the women he's going to try to pick up using the picture of us.

Fifteen minutes later and we're on our way home. Thankfully the minivan is drivable.

"Guess who got a date?" Sky holds up her cell phone and places it in the cup holder. "See yah GeekMatch, hello handcuffs."

I shoot her a tight smile. "Mind if we head home? I need to rest my arm."

"Sure. No problem."

Her enthusiasm tapers down and I feel like the jackass I am.

CHAPTER TEN

Mount Me and Skylar go out that Friday. I refrained from leaving my room, lying and saying I wasn't feeling good. I booted up my laptop one handed and almost bought a ticket home to Park City. It seems like it might be a better option than putting myself through this crap. Maybe some distance wouldn't make it feel like someone is prying my fingernails off one by one.

She could have her happy white picket fence and I could live my own life. We could remain friends via phone calls and Skype sessions. I'd endure the wedding, the children's birthday parties all in moderation. Maybe after she became a casualty of the sixty percent divorce rate, I could move in with her and help her care for her kids. Perfect scenario—a little demented and selfish on my part, but she'd still be in my life and I'd be with her in a manner of speaking.

A knock on my bedroom door just after eleven tells me her date didn't go as well as she was hoping when she left.

"Come in."

She peeks her head in just like she did on her last date, like she's afraid of what she might encounter.

Did she think I'd be beating off? Hell, I wanted to, especially after I booted up my laptop. Turns out I'm not ambidextrous. My left hand just can't get the motion right. Which explains even more why being around Skylar lately feels like a form of sexual torture—one where the relief never actually comes. Literally and figuratively.

She slides in next to me in bed, her eyes shifting from my bare chest to her legs, crossing her ankles.

"You're home early. Does that mean no cuffing?"

She giggles, though it sounds forced. "Turns out police officers can be kind of bossy."

"Who would have thought?" I deadpan.

She knocks her shoulder into mine, leaning her head there after, her dark hair falling over my bare skin. It tickles a bit and it reminds me of what her fingertips might feel like brushing across my chest.

"He ordered for me," she says.

I clench my jaw and widen my eyes.

"Yeah."

"Sorry, he was a hottie, too."

She slaps my stomach and the only reason I'm joking around is because her date went badly. If she'd come in here tomorrow morning dressed in what she wore tonight, I'd be clenching my fists instead of laughing.

"He was good looking. Oh." She inches back, resting her back on the headboard. "Turns out not everyone is impressed by what we do. He asked me why I would ever want to twirl up in the air and risk injury."

"Really? Usually people think we're badass."

She giggles, the true, real kind of laugh I'm used to. "I know, right? I guess Officer Stick Up His Ass likes control."

"Not surprising since he's sworn to uphold the law and all."

"I guess I was kind of blind on that one, huh?"

"Maybe, since he got your number *and* still gave you a ticket for the accident." I quirk an eyebrow and she shrugs, agreeing with me.

"How are you feeling?" she asks, changing the subject. Man, am I ever glad she never dated seriously in Park City. It's mentally exhausting. She's O for two right now.

"Better." Truth is, I never felt bad.

She bites her lip and stares over at me. Her signature tell, letting me know that she wants to ask me something she doesn't think I'll agree to.

"What?"

"It's still early and I haven't showed you any of the clubs in Chicago. What do you say?"

"I say, I have a broken arm and I'm in my pajamas." I raise my sling up a bit away from my body.

She tugs at my arm. "Come on. I'll protect your arm. I'm all dressed up and I want to make the best of what turned out to be a dud of a night."

Standing up now, I realize that her dress is more revealing than when she went out with Tad.

How can I really say no to her when she's looking at me like that?

"Fine, let me get dressed," I mumble.

She jumps up and down, clapping her hands. "Thanks. I'll go call us an Uber and who knows, maybe Chels will want to join us."

Gee, wouldn't that be great. I ask the big man upstairs for a small favor hoping that Chelsea has a date.

CHELSEA DID NOT HAVE A DATE.

"Awesome." Chelsea peeks her head out from inside the club over the bouncer who could probably knock me out with one swing. I'm aware at how pussy that sounds, but obviously, in Chicago, they make the guys big. "They're with me, Adrian." She pats his arm.

He smiles down at her. Yeah, he's being this polite because he wants in her pants. Not that I give a shit as long as I'm not waiting in the line wrapping around the corner.

"Thanks." Skylar smiles up at the bouncer.

"She competed in the Winter Classics." Chelsea points to Sky and the bouncer smiles down at her again with those lovesick eyes. "And this is her friend Beckett." The guy gives me the signature guy-to-guy nod.

We head into the club and its dark with an array of strobe lights flickering down across the bodies on the dance floor. I tightened my sling on the Uber ride, so it was closer to my chest. I'm sure I've gone against doctor orders, but if I had to sit in that house one more minute and stare at the Leave It to Beaver childhood home I'd go crazy.

I love the Walshes, in my eyes, they're the perfect family. And maybe it's the fact Skylar is thinking about staying here, or that her womb has some sudden urgency to want to hold a baby and her left ring finger feels too light without a diamond ring. All of that shit is suffocating me. Now that we're at a club, this is where I can let all that go.

"Come on." Chelsea waves us through the wall to wall people. Skylar's gaze shoots to me over her shoulder. I follow, reluctantly though since I'd much rather have it be just me and Skylar here.

We stop in front of a table full of chicks. *Great.*

"This is my cousin, Skylar and her friend, Beckett." We stand on the outside of the circular booth, three other girls staring up at us. The blonde in the middle blatantly checks me out.

Chelsea grabs the waitress, ordering us a round of shots. Skylar's smile is beaming as bright as the spotlights on the dance floor. The blond is imagining eating me with a fucking spoon. Chelsea's busy chatting with everyone that walks by and the way the blonde woman is looking at me like she's imagining eating me up with a spoon is making me uncomfortable.

"Let's dance," I whisper in Skylar's ear.

She nods, telling Chelsea that we'll be back. Chelsea nods, looking past Skylar and giving me that whole 'I'm watching you signal' with her fingers pointing to her eyes and then to me.

What the fuck ever.

I lead Skylar out to the dance floor, letting the people swallow us up so we're away from Chelsea's prying eyes. The base thumping through the speakers has the dance floor practically shaking.

We've danced plenty in clubs. We're no strangers to each other's bodies, so when I place my thigh between her legs I don't expect much to happen. I definitely didn't expect my dick to go half chub, or have Skylar bridge the distance so we would be chest-to-chest if it weren't for this damn sling. We usually do our pretend dirty dancing that makes us laugh, rarely taking ourselves seriously on the dance floor. Neither one of us about to win any contests.

I can't say if it's the song, or warm bodies swarmed around us, but this time we're not laughing. A light sheen of sweat covers our bodies as we grind together. Skylar's eyes are fixed on mine and I can't look away. My hand slides up her side, her body molding closer to me.

She's warm and soft in my arms, the smell of her

perfume intoxicating me. I turn her in my arms so that her back is to my chest and though nothing feels more natural than us on the outside of the friend zone, I know we're playing with fire. Have we *both* been fighting this thing growing between us so hard that after only one song, my dick is grinding into her ass?

Her body tenses, her back stiffening as my lips hover on top of her shoulder. Just one taste my internal demon tells me. See if she's as sweet as you imagine. He continues to taunt me.

The last thing I want is her to pull away, so I lay my hand on her flat stomach and she wraps her hand over mine as though she's saying we're on the same page.

Her chest rises and falls and not because of the strenuous dance moves we're doing. It's happening. The inevitable crossover from friends to lovers and I came unprepared because my body's humming yes, yes when my mind should be overriding it. Tonight, I don't want to think about reason or think about the consequences of our actions. I just want one swipe of my tongue along her shoulder. One taste of her lips.

My mouth is millimeters away from her skin, my fingers brushing the stray hairs away. As if the devil is punishing me for taking too long, someone runs into my back and I lose my footing, unable to hold onto Skylar with only one arm. She falls to the ground, her knee catching the stage from the DJ's area.

I look behind me to see if I can catch the fucker who bumped us, but either their long gone or smart enough to act like nothing is amiss. Seconds later, I hold my hand out to her, not missing the sight of blood trickling down her leg.

"Come on."

She takes my hand and I get her back to the booth.

"What did you do?" Chelsea says, dipping a napkin in a water glass and placing it on her cousin's leg.

Skylar tosses back the shot sitting on the table. "I think I'm ready to go home."

Chelsea gives me a look like this is my fault.

"Let's go. I'll get a taxi home," I snip, both annoyed and grateful for the interruption.

Skylar stands, giving Chelsea a hug goodbye and then I guide her out of the building.

I can't help but think that fate is calling the shots now. Sometimes we all need saving from ourselves.

CHAPTER ELEVEN

Two days later, Skylar and I walk into some deli to meet Chelsea for lunch. She stands when she sees us, frantically raising her hand like we'd miss her in the small downtown lunch spot.

"Hey." Skylar frees herself from her jacket and sits down at the table.

"I didn't know you were bringing him." She looks me up and down, unimpressed.

"Him? Do you have amnesia? You know my name." I don't bother taking off my jacket because it's more trouble than it's worth and I'm not planning on staying long.

"We were coming from a doctor's appointment," Skylar says, hanging her jacket off the back of the chair.

"I'll gladly leave," I comment, and Chelsea shoots me a look that says yes please.

She glances over my shoulder for a second and then her narrowed eyes widen, a smile overtaking her entire face. "No, it's okay. Stay."

"Stay?" I ask.

Skylar's busy looking around the place and then she

suddenly grabs my arm, her fingers digging into my flesh even over my jacket.

"Whoa, let's keep this my good arm." I slide it out from under her.

She doesn't glance over at me, instead she slides closer, her voice low. "It's Layla Andrews," she whisper shouts.

The name sounds familiar, but I can't place it. Please tell me this isn't another fucking friend that's going to put her back in her feeling bad about herself depression.

"Hello, that's why I summoned you here." Chelsea glances over, and waves.

"You know her? Is that the manny guy?" Skylar who obviously hasn't let her US Weekly subscription wane sounds like she's about to scream and attack the poor woman with two kids hanging off her.

"Yes and YES!" Chelsea leans back. "The magazines did not do him justice. Wait until you see his ass."

The woman—Layla—waves back and they make their way over.

"Well, I have nothing better to do all day." Skylar leans back, her legs kicked out in front of her with her ankles crossed.

I glance over to get another look at the guy. I don't know what Sky's going on about. He looks average to me.

"Who are they?" I ask, mindlessly picking up the plastic triangle thing in the middle of the table with the specials and an advertisement for Tavern Meats on it.

"Put the Powder magazine down once in awhile, Beckett. It's Layla Andrews and her boyfriend." Chelsea says this like I'm an idiot for not knowing it already.

"I thought you said he was the manny?"

"Jeez Beckett, come back down to Earth."

I stand, figuring while I'm here I might as well get a

sandwich. Just as I move, Skylar grabs my wrist, stopping me.

"Why are they here?" she whispers.

Chelsea leans over the table. "My new boss is funding his script and Layla is the star. They have a meeting with her and wanted lunch. She already had something on her calendar for lunch and we've yet to hire her an assistant, so guess who she asked?" She's beaming.

"Oprah?" I guess.

Chelsea rolls her eyes.

"I'm so jelly you have connections like this. Who is this woman you're working for?"

"I'm getting a sandwich." I glance down to my wrist that still has Skylar's hand around it.

"Sorry. Yeah, I was stopping you from leaving."

"I wish I could, but you're my driver. Want anything?"

Skylar looks over her shoulder to the chalkboard behind the case full of artery clogging meats.

"I'll be there in a minute."

The case is filled with sandwich meats that I've never even seen before and from the names of them, I'm assuming they're Italian. As I wait in the line, I investigate why a place with a Chicago flag painted on one wall and pictures galore is named simply The Sandwich Place.

The line moves quickly and most of the patrons are dressed in suits or dresses. Women in heels with fashion computer bags hung from their arms with phones pressed to their ears.

A woman about my age is at the register. A soft smile plays on her lips when I step forward, a pad of paper in her hand. "What can I get you?"

I check the chalkboard to see what number I want from

the thirty different sandwiches they offer. "I'll have the thirteen."

She jots it down. "Chips, drink, cannoli?"

"Drink, no chips and maybe I'll be back for cannoli."

She places the pad down, ringing me up, her pleasant smile turning coy. "I can't promise they'll be any left. They're our specialty."

Normally, I'd lean over the counter, give her some lame line asking if she's on the menu. She'd giggle, I'd say how I just got back from the Classics and casually throw in how I claimed silver. Hell, I might even exaggerate, okay lie, about my injured arm. But what happened a few nights ago with Skylar is still fresh in my mind. Something has shifted. The fact that I keep my good hand in my pocket when we're near says how uncomfortable things have become between us. The last two mornings, she's showered and dressed before coming downstairs.

When we arrived home from the club that night I grabbed her mom's first aid kid from the laundry room, bandaged her up, and watched her go to bed. It was all I could do not to follow.

That's when that damn light bulb in my head not only lit up, it shined like a fucking spotlight. Our relationship, er, friendship was on the cusp of collapse and I needed to do something to keep that from happening.

"What did you get?" Skylar peeks her head over my shoulder.

"The Italian one." I point up to the board.

She laughs and pats my stomach from behind. "You do realize that sooner or later you'll have to watch your diet."

"You know I commit to a full year of eating whatever I want."

Not really, because I wouldn't grab any air to do my

tricks if I had a gut the size of most middle-aged husbands, but it's only been a few weeks. Skylar should be living it up, too.

"Splurge," I say, and her arm doesn't leave my stomach.

The cashier is eyeing the closeness between us.

"Okay." Skylar rushes over to stand in front of the cashier before a line forms again.

I let a relieved breath go now that her hand isn't on my body any longer.

A minute later, she's got her number and is standing next to me again.

"You're not going to ask for an autograph?" I eye the celebrity couple and their kids clearing off their table. The boy's pretending he's flying an airplane from his coloring page, weaving up and down the rows of tables.

The little girl pulls down her mom's blouse, exposing part of her bra. The man, rushing over, murmurs something to the woman. She laughs and he buttons up her blouse, snatching the baby from her arms. I watch for no reason other than fascination because the guy looks like he's having the time of his life. She rises up on her toes, placing one hand on his cheek and bringing her lips to his other cheek. He circles his hand around her waist, pulling her as close as he can and the two sneak in an inappropriate kiss, although my stalker self might be the only one who saw it.

A hand waves in front of my face. "I think maybe you're the one who wants the autograph." Skylar giggles and I snap back to attention.

Two days ago, that scene wouldn't have warmed my insides. I need to get the hell out of Chicago.

A cold rush of winter air ignites goose bumps along my neck and Skylar and I both turn our heads, but it's not the celebrity couple that catches our eye as they leave.

"Holy..." Skylar's voice breaks, but her gaze doesn't shift.

A man walks in, and yeah, I'll reluctantly admit that he might be what some girls would call hot. He rounds the case of meat and heads to the back of the shop, the scent of cologne drowning my nostrils in his wake.

"Obviously knows the owners," I mumble, sparing a glance at Skylar, who practically has drool running down her chin.

"Whoa," she says, looking more star struck than she did a bit ago when she saw the actual fucking movie star and then heads back to the table.

I chuckle the emptiest laugh I've ever had, trying to play it off.

"Mama!" The man's voice booms out from the back and through the entire place.

"Mauro." A woman's voice follows, sweet and endearing and rolling the r in his name.

A twinge of jealousy stabs my insides. It's funny how you can tell so much by the way someone says a person's name. There's no denying she loves her son.

The two start talking in a language I don't understand. Italian is my best guess.

"Number forty-three," the man—Mauro I guess—says, and places my sandwich on the counter in a black basket with wax paper made to look like a newspaper.

Skylar's next to Chelsea when I reach the table. She's obviously decided to wait for her number to be called here instead of by the counter, which relieves me since I try to avoid being alone with Chelsea as much as possible.

"Oh, it looks awesome." Skylar stares at my sandwich much the same way she did the guy who came in moments ago.

"Yeah, Chelsea had a good pick for once." I push my straw through the lid on my cup.

She shoots me an annoyed look that distorts her face unattractively. "As I was saying," Chelsea pauses for dramatic flare. "He's one of their sons. There's three of them, and hand to God, each one is just as hot."

"And you haven't snagged one of them up?" Skylar asks, twirling her number in her hand.

Chelsea waves her hand and I look back over my shoulder to see the guy approaching our table.

"They're Italian, Sky. Old school possessive mama. Too much drama for me." She rises from her chair and is enveloped in the guy's arms.

"Chels, how'd I miss you when I walked in?" His blue eyes spark when they land on Skylar.

I thought Italians all had brown eyes?

The douchebag needs to keep it moving. Maybe go visit his mama again.

"You tell me," Chelsea responds in a flirty voice.

The two of them laugh and suddenly my sandwich nauseates me.

"This is my cousin, Skylar Walsh, she just got back from the Classics."

His eyes widen.

Yeah, yeah, yeah, we know, it's amazing, you're impressed, whatever.

He holds his hand out to her.

"Mauro Bianco," he says, and the last name triggers my memory of the car accident. It can't be a coincidence.

"Nice to meet you." Skylar's voice is low and sultry as her body falls to the back of the chair like saying hello took all of her energy.

I'd like to smack the smile off Mauro's face because it's

not a 'nice to meet you smile,' it's a 'can I dip my hands down your pants and feel how wet I made you' smile.

"Hey," he shifts his attention to me and nods.

"Beckett."

"This is Skylar's *friend*," Chelsea adds.

He scrutinizes me, his brows furrowing. "You look so familiar."

"Do you happen to be related to a cop and a paramedic?" I ask.

Skylar glances over at me, shocked. Oh, that's right, she was consumed with her conversation with Officer Mount Me during the entire exchange after the accident.

Mauro snaps his fingers and points to me, recognition lighting his face.

"Duh," Chelsea says and points to the painted wall, split into three parts. One has the Chicago Police Department symbol with the chequered pattern on top and bottom in the middle. The firefighter symbol with flames on its left and the paramedic symbol on it's right, equally loved with a painted ambulance.

Mauro laughs. "What can I say, my parents are proud." He shrugs, but the smile adorning his face says he's happy about that. "You're a snowboarder, right?"

I nod.

"My brother Luca showed his picture with you to the entire bar. You may be responsible for some little Bianco's in about nine months."

I laugh.

"Number forty-eight," the young girl behind the counter calls out.

Skylar moves to stand, but Mauro presses his hand on her shoulder. "I got it."

She falls back down into the chair, clutching her chest

and heaving for a breath. Okay, maybe I'm exaggerating slightly, but she definitely likes him.

A minute later, Skylar's sandwich is placed in front of her. "Good choice on the cannoli. Homemade." He winks and for fuck's sake if she was an ice cream cone she'd be a puddle on the floor because she practically melts back into her seat.

"Is it your day off?" Chelsea asks.

"I'm on in a few hours."

"I'm guessing you're the firefighter?" I ask, biting my sandwich.

"What a brainiac you are," Chelsea says, sparing me a glance.

Mauro looks down at her, probably wondering why she's so snarky to me, especially since I've tapered down my own reaction toward her. We're in public after all.

"Yeah. I'm the oldest so I think they followed in my footsteps, each thinking they could outdo me. Hello, I run into burning buildings." You can tell he's joking, that he's really not full of himself and if it wasn't for the way his gaze keeps shifting back toward Skylar, I'd probably like the guy, but not when he likes her.

Mauro sits down at our table and I internally groan. "So, Skylar, my brother told me you went out with his partner?"

Skylar sips her drink, her sandwich still untouched. "Yeah." Her eyes flicker to me. "A few nights ago."

"How'd that go?" He leans back in his chair, his muscular arms crossing over his chest.

"He was nice." She shrugs and shifts in her seat.

"Nice?" He raises his eyebrows. "That's not the usual adjective someone would use to describe Michaels."

She giggles, her fingers knotting in her lap in front of her. "Well, I was trying to be polite."

Mauro sits up straighter, links his hands on top of the table, leaning over like Chelsea and I aren't here. "No need. The guy is a tool."

She laughs some more and my insides churn watching this scene play out.

"You know what?" Chelsea stands. "This sounds impromptu, but why don't Beckett and I give you two some space."

Skylar doesn't refuse and either does Mauro, their eyes still fixated on each other.

Fucking Chelsea.

But what am I supposed to do? I stand, collect my sandwich and drink, and I'm not even sitting at the other table before Mauro slides over into my seat beside Skylar.

From three tables over, I watch the woman I'm just figuring out I love more than a friend, twist her hair and laugh at another man's jokes. As usual in my life, I've been set aside.

CHAPTER TWELVE

"You don't mind, right Beckett?" Chelsea leans back in her chair, her legs crossed as she types away on her phone.

"Don't you have a job?"

"What do you think I'm doing right now?" She flips her phone my way, but I don't bother looking.

I take a bite of my sandwich. I'll fight through the rolling emotions inside making my stomach rumble with turmoil.

"So, you don't mind if Mauro and Skylar go out, right? Just think of the beautiful babies they'll make together."

I don't respond. I know she's trying to get a rise out of me. Everything in me tells me to get up, grab Sky and kiss her until Mauro is lost in a sea of black behind me.

"Cut it." I push a perfectly mouth-watering sandwich aside, my eyes shifting between the sandwich and them.

Chelsea's conniving laugh is all I hear as I try to shift my attention away from Skylar and Mauro. His mom walks out from behind the counter, stopping in her tracks and then smiles, continuing forward. Then as she cleans up some of the tables, it's me *and* her stealing looks at the happy couple.

He's perfect for Skylar. A firefighter, which means he thinks of others before himself. Seems to come from a big happy family just like hers. And the kicker, he lives in Chicago where she wants to go to grad school. As I stack up the comparisons, a small part of me withers and dies because he's the perfect man for her. Far more perfect than me.

A phone rings and everyone, including Skylar glances at his or her phones. Mauro's mom walks fast toward the corded phone on the wall. She answers and that smiling face turns into a frown. Not even waiting until she's off the phone, she plucks a cell phone out of the front pocket of her apron. I laugh when I read the case that says 'It's not a party until my Italian meatballs come out' written in red, white and green.

She hangs up the phone, presses two buttons on her cell and her face turns redder the longer it takes. The person must answer because she starts rambling in Italian, mixing in a few English words.

"Luca!" she scolds and I'm guessing that's the same Luca I met after the accident—the paramedic.

"Don't 'Mama me,' stop giving out the deli number to your girls." She pauses before her face softens a little.

"Luca, Il diavolo fa le pentole ma non i coperchi!"

She clicks the phone off.

Mauro excuses himself and goes over to his mother where the two continue speaking in Italian. Mauro's unable to hide his humor at his brother's antics.

His mom points to Skylar's back, waggling her eyebrows. Mauro's gaze shoots to me and I bury my head in my phone.

A minute later, he and Skylar are standing at the edge of our table. The chair squeaks as I rise from my seat. Usually, I have some height on guys, but Mauro is eye to eye with me.

"Your mom didn't seem very happy." I shake my head, amused at the woman.

He chuckles. "My brother, Luca, the paramedic." He waits for me to acknowledge. "He gives his one-night stands the deli number. She's tired of it, says he'll die alone."

"What did she say in Italian?" Chelsea asks.

Mauro rolls his eyes. "The closest English translation would be what goes around comes around. That one day, a girl will do what he does to them. Luca is...well, let's say he's not ready to settle down yet."

"Might as well live it up while he can, right?" I say.

Mauro says nothing. Apparently, I'm the only one of us four who doesn't feel worthy of committing to one person. Maybe I should give Luca a call.

"I gotta go. Nice meeting you." I stick out my left hand and he takes it skeptically. I should've just shot him a head nod instead of this left-handed grip.

"Sorry, for the godfather handshake, but as you can tell," I lift my sling, "the dangers of being a silver medalist snowboarder have me as a bit of a gimp at the moment."

"Or those pesky well-placed ice patches," Chelsea adds.

I narrow my eyes and she smiles brightly up at me. I'd like to strap her to my board and send her down a mountain.

"Costs of the job, right?" Mauro says.

"Did I mention that Mauro is a firefighter for our fine city?" Chelsea's smile shifts from sweet to sinister.

No one says anything since that was established earlier.

"Yeah, he runs into burning buildings and you ride a

board down a hill. Definitely comparable on the danger level," she continues.

Again, I give her my best icy glare. I'd like to see her break fifteen bones in her body and get back up to do it again. I'm fairly sure taking a celebrity family to lunch and making bullshit calls for someone doesn't get your adrenaline pumping.

"Oh, Chels," Mauro says. "I can't imagine being a professional athlete. The schedule must be grueling." He's not looking to me when he says it though, his gaze is set on Skylar.

She gives him that shy smile. The one that suggests she isn't a firecracker under her delicate features.

"Don't you guys always have enormous meals or some shit at the firehouse? Sky and I live on plant life most of the time and lean proteins."

The Italian stallion smiles.

"Right Sky? Remember that time we pigged out on take-out after the X Games?" I ask her.

Skylar softens her smile for me and then looks up to Mauro, nodding. She acts like I'm her little sister and she's tolerating me so she doesn't get grounded, otherwise she can't go to the party Saturday night.

"You do learn how to cook if you're a fireman," Mauro agrees.

"A man who saves lives *and* can cook. Do you clean, too? And how close are you to your mother?" Skylar elbows Chelsea, her cheeks growing redder the longer we stand here.

"That might be my downfall. I have a housecleaner and I'm Italian, so the mother thing is self-explanatory."

All three of them laugh and I feel like the loser at a party who doesn't get the inside joke. He just openly admitted he's a momma's boy. I bet his Italian mother still does his laundry and cuts up his meat for him. At least with me, Skylar wouldn't have to deal with in-laws, I'm a party of one.

"Housecleaners are good, too," Chelsea says.

Will she ever just shut up? She's practically writing this guy's want ad and trying to match him with Skylar. Who is she, the Match.com spokesperson?

"I better get going. My shift starts at three," Mauro says, rubbing the back of his neck with his hand.

I search out a clock and like I assumed, there's one perfectly placed on the wall over top of the deli counter. *Two o'clock.* This guy must've really wanted to stick around to talk to Skylar. Who wouldn't?

"I'll walk you out," Skylar says, and steps through our mini circle.

"Nice to meet you." He nods at me. "Chelsea," he says, following Skylar. Probably checking her ass out.

"Oh. My. God." Chelsea clasps her heart, her hand squeezing the edge of the table for support.

"Dramatic much?"

She stands up straight, rolls her eyes. "He's drop-dead gorgeous. Did you see his bicep muscles straining his shirt sleeves, or the corded muscles flexing in his forearm?"

"Forearms? Seriously?"

She slaps me on the back. "Forearms are sexy as fuck, Beck."

"A dick is sexy as fuck, Chelsea."

An older couple that just came in turns back to look at me and then to Chelsea. *Shit.*

"Sorry," I mumble to the couple. "Want some dessert? It's on me."

The man smiles and shakes his head while the woman's

gaze concentrates on my crotch like she's sizing me up. I oddly want to cover my junk with my hands. This is how women must feel when us men are being pigs.

"You." Chelsea points to me, bending her finger for me to follow her.

Why? So, I can hear how fucking great, Marco, Maurice or whatever the fuck his name is?

My gaze flickers outside. The two of them both have their phones out. Great, they're exchanging numbers now. Chelsea will probably get a promotion at Match.com now for her set-up of the perfect couple.

"Beckett." This time Chelsea's voice is sterner. It reminds me of one of my foster mom's where if we still didn't listen, all hell broke loose.

I head in her direction of the cashier. Chelsea ordered a to-go tray of cannoli dip and broken rolls. Of course she did.

She slaps me on the back. "Pay the woman."

I hand my credit card to the cashier and she rings me up and hands me the slip to sign without her earlier smile.

I get Mauro looks like a model in a fitness magazine, but I'm not too shabby either. I have a killer career and that stubble/beard thing that all the women these days seem to like. I'm a catch, too, damn it.

But like I have to keep reminding myself—I'm not Skylar's to catch. I'm not anyone's really.

CHAPTER THIRTEEN

Game night at the Walshes is no joke—running tallies, razzing and competitiveness that put me, Grady and Dax to shame. I've seen Zoe in tears, I've seen Skylar punch her brother in the shoulder. The Walshes are ruthless and as much as they laugh during these nights, they bicker, too. It fascinated me at first until I realized it's survival of the fittest. I don't cry, and her brother and I don't fight, but Skylar didn't talk to me for a week once. Long story.

Skylar's putting out the chips and her mom's seven-layer taco dip, while I've made sure the fridge is stocked with beer. The door opens, and I wait to hear the thumping of little footsteps, but Zoe and Vin round the corner with a brown grocery bag and a case of beer.

"What's this?" Skylar rears back from the table, surprise written all over her face.

"We're kid-free!" Zoe starts shaking her hips and then her and Vin start grinding with the bag between them.

"Aw, I'd rented some kid's movies and everything." Skylar hurries over and takes the bag from her sister's arms.

"Vin's parents wanted them for a night and who are we

to deny them their wonderfully well-behaved grandchildren." She cocks her eye to Vin who looks like he's about a second from laughing.

"They helped mold them," he adds, raising the case of beer in his hand. Alpha Beer, the Greek beer he says grows thicker hair on your chest. Must work for your back, too, based on the time Vin and I hit the hot tub when they visited in Utah.

Vin and I take a seat in the adjoining living room while Zoe and Skylar continue preparations in the kitchen. The two of them are laughing off and on and I can't help but think how since she met Mauro, Skylar's been in a good mood. I have no idea if they've talked or texted, and part of me wishes her phone would malfunction and lose just his number altogether.

"Hello, hello!" Chelsea walks in with a bag full of liquor. "I heard a rumor." She stops in the middle of the room, looking right and left. She holds her finger to her lips and we all play her little game of keeping quiet. "Adult night!" her hips slide from side to side as her knees bend and she moves down and twists back up. "It's party time!"

"Great," I mumble, getting rewarded with a carrot thrown at my forehead. I pick it up and chomp down on it while looking at Zoe. "Who brought this nutritious crap into the house?"

Zoe smirks and the front door opens again.

Skylar's brother, Mike waltzes in. Now here's a guy I like. Carefree, just moved into downtown on his own. He brings a different girl to every game night that I've been to and although Skylar's mom always acts like the random girl could be the one, everyone else is well aware she isn't.

"Mikey!" Vin and I yell in unison.

He holds up a bottle of tequila in one hand, a bag of limes in the other. "I heard there's a party here tonight?"

We all look on, waiting for some shy girl to join him at his side, but no one comes.

"What gives?" Chelsea asks, looking behind him into the hallway.

Mikey shakes his head. "I'm flying solo. Guess you can be my partner tonight." He wraps his arm around his cousin's shoulder.

"Who says I don't have a date coming?" she mocks offense. Chelsea would never bring a guy around. As much as she likes to throw stones, she was already married once and from the little that Sky says about it, it failed spectacularly.

"Is Mr. Snuggles here?" Mikey does his best kiddie voice and Chelsea shoves him, joining Sky and Zoe in the kitchen.

Mikey walks over to Vin and me, giving us each a handshake. "Who's Mr. Snuggles?" I ask.

"It's a stuffed animal from when we were little. I may have hidden it from her numerous times." He shrugs. "One time she cried so hard she threw up."

We laugh, but we don't have a lot of time at the bar getting drinks before the girls are preparing a card game.

"We've got a new one for you boys tonight." Zoe waves a box in the air and all I catch is the word Meme.

Mikey snaps his finger and points. "And my friends asked why I'd come here on a Saturday night."

"Without the kids peering over the shoulders and with Mom and Dad in Arizona we can have some real fun," Zoe says.

"Shit, what kind of game is it?" Vin asks and we all take

our spots around the table. Skylar on my left and thankfully Mikey—not Chelsea—on my right.

"Hey, I heard I missed you guys last weekend?" Mikey sips his beer and glances over. "I also heard the dance floor was hot." He raises his eyebrows a few times.

Chelsea laughs next to him. Neither Skylar nor I look at each other or react. We still haven't talked about that night. Thankfully, Zoe's already down to business and begins to explain the game to us.

"Okay, I pick a card with a picture on it and then you each are going to pick a line to go with it from the cards you get so that you make a meme." Zoe passes out the cards.

"Shit, Zo," Skylar stares down at her selection of phrases to use for the picture.

"It's like caption, but you have to use the cards you're given. I'll read them through and pick the winner based on which one is the funniest. Then that person grabs a meme and we do the whole thing over until we finish and whoever has the most meme pictures wins."

We all nod in understanding.

Zoe puts down a picture of a man sitting back on his couch with his hands linked behind his head, his feet up on the coffee table.

We each put down our caption face down and Zoe picks them up, reading them out loud. "When you invite them over to Netflix and chill when you know you don't have Netflix."

The table laughs because it was the funniest one.

"That's a bad thing?" Mikey asks. "I never get any complaints."

Both sisters roll their eyes, Zoe grabbing a pretzel and throwing it at him. "You're such a manwhore."

"Manwhore? They know what they sign up for, sis."

Zoe shakes her head, passing the meme cards to Chelsea since she picked the winning caption. She looks through the heavy stack and Skylar's phone lights up between us.

She quickly presses the side to make the screen go black. As if that move wasn't bad enough she glances quickly to the side to check if I saw her.

"Who's that?" I ask, tossing a pretzel into my mouth and hoping to appear more casual than I feel right now.

She picks up her phone and puts it on do not disturb. "No one."

"Bullshit," Mikey coughs out.

"Mauro?" Chelsea raises her eyebrows.

I wish red wasn't the first color that falls like a curtain over my eyes. Followed seconds later by green.

"Who's Mauro?" Mikey asks.

"A firefighter she met. Super hot," Chelsea adds in her unwanted two cents.

"Why don't you pick a card?" I say to her and she rolls her eyes, a smirk on her lips.

"Here." She places a meme of two confused kids with their hands up in the air. "Happy?"

"Yes." I look through my caption cards and put down the one I select.

Vin's taking a while, so I grab a handful of pretzels and lean back.

"Is it? Mauro?" I ask even though I know I need to let this shit go.

Skylar nods, but never makes eye contact with me.

The table grows quiet and I feel like there's a spotlight over my head while everyone waits to see how I react.

"He seemed cool," I say and shrug, feigning nonchalance.

Chelsea roots through all the caption cards and starts

laughing. "This is so the winner...When you ask for directions and the dickhead uses east and west."

We all laugh and the tension from moments ago evaporates.

For the next hour, the meme game turns into a tequila shot drinking game for everyone who doesn't get his or her caption picked.

I blame Mikey.

Two hours later, the memes and the captions are thrown on the kitchen table as more and more people arrive with alcohol in their hands and party time in their head.

Three hours later, I'm cornered, alone in the kitchen with Skylar, trying to remember why I keep insisting it isn't a good idea for the two of us to be together.

CHAPTER FOURTEEN

"So, what's up with you and Mauro?" I ask, my tequila laced breath blowing down on Skylar.

We're tucked in the pantry with a party roaring to life outside. I don't even remember how we ended up in here alone. I think she came in looking for a snack and I followed like a lost puppy.

"Why do you care?" She sways slightly but grips the wire racks before losing her balance.

I'd catch her if she was falling, but she probably doesn't believe I would.

"Because you're my friend."

She rolls her eyes.

"What's that?" I point to her eyes. "You're always rolling your eyes at me lately."

She lightly shoves me away, her hand moving to the pantry door. "Don't."

"Sky?" Her name coming as more of a plea in my tone. "What's the problem?"

She whips around, and I almost forgot how snarky she can get when she drinks. I move more toward the lover part of my personality and she takes a hard right into the fighter portion of hers.

"You tell me, Beckett. This," she waves a finger between the two of us, "we're just friends, right? Well, then Mauro is no business of yours."

"Whoa, whoa, whoa, Sky. No need to be mean." I sip the beer in my hands. No idea how many I've had. "I was just curious."

"No, you want to piss around me in a circle. What do you want, Beckett? You want me to remain single my entire life, so we can be best friends? Well, as much as you like life to stand still, it doesn't. The Earth still spins on its axis daily."

"Are you giving me a science class right now?"

She takes a bag of rice and throws it at me. I move to the side just in time and the little grains sprinkle all over the floor.

When I look up, she's gone.

Fuck.

I follow her, but it seems like the size of the party has doubled in the short time I cornered her. I swear every one of their friends from high school is here. Chelsea's dancing on the coffee table, Mikey's throwing back shots with a group of guys around his dad's bar, but Zoe and Vin aren't in sight and I'd bet money they left based on the make-out session they were having before I went into the kitchen.

"Beckett!" Chelsea screams, pointing to me, effectively making everyone around her glance my way.

My gaze moves away from Skylar's retreating back to her.

"You know I love you, right? I give you a lot of shit, but secretly..." she motions between the two of us with her finger. "We enjoy giving each other hell."

"I think you're drunk."

She smiles, and then a new song comes on and she's swaying her hips. "I know I'm drunk!"

How the hell did this party get so out of hand?

"Beck, come take a shot." Mikey motions me over.

He pulls me into him with an arm around my neck. "This guy will be my brother-in-law one day."

The other guys say nothing and I'm not going to embarrass him by saying I'm not. What once felt like any easy punch line now makes it feel like I've been punched in the gut.

"He can get whatever ass he wants, but he's faithful to my sister even when he's not getting it from her." He pushes me back by my chest.

Shit, is that how it's perceived? That I get more action with my hand than women? I don't care from an ego point of view, but do they all think I've been pining away for Skylar for four years?

"You're telling me you've got a Classics medal. You're on television and not bad looking." One of his friends steps up alongside me. "And you're not getting regular ass?"

I lift my arm. "I gotta a broken arm."

The guy slaps me on the back. "Hell, if I were you, I'd still be out living it up. Go for what you want and to hell with the consequences." He points to my sling.

Mikey slides a shot glass in front of me. "Fuck yeah." He raises his own glass in the air and all his friends do the same. "Always go for what you want."

Mikey waits for me to raise my glass, but I'm still processing the words from his friend. Why the hell am I not taking what I want because she's going to leave me anyway? She's got plans for grad school, to stay here in Chicago and she obviously wants to date other people. Can one night really ruin us?

I knock back the shot and slam the glass down on the table. On my way out of the room, Chelsea screams, "Who wants to go out to the bar?"

Good. Because what I'm about to do needs some privacy.

Lucky for me, the entire party is in agreement, and everyone starts hollering about who's going to ping the Ubers and how many they need.

Walking up the stairs, I glance down to see people putting on their jackets and shoes. Chelsea's gaze raises to mine and she winks. "I'll be sure to lock up."

I don't respond. Instead, I walk down the hall and knock on the only closed door.

"Yeah," Sky says from the other side.

My palm stretches over the knob and I close my eyes and try to put my drunken thoughts in order. When I open the door, she's laying on her bed, her phone raised above her head, the screen the only light in the room.

"Everyone is going to the bar," I say.

"You go. I'm staying home," she says, not bothering to glance my way.

"I'm not going anywhere."

My tone must be my tell because she springs up, her phone laying at her side, her eyes widened in surprise. "Why not?"

"Because I'm going to do something I should've done a long time ago."

I shut the door and step forward where I fall on my knees in front of her. Using my left hand, I pull her toward me by her neck and release all the pent up sexual tension between us.

My lips meet hers and a moan sounds between us, but I'm not sure if it was her or me. Her lips are as warm and soft as I imagined. Both her hands cradle my cheeks and I don't want to sound like a chick, but an overwhelming feeling of peace and safety consumes me.

I crave more—more of her touch, more of her lips, more of her sweetness—more everything. It's clear how much she has to offer if she were more than a friend. Damn, if I don't hope she is feeling the same way I am.

I inwardly curse my one-arm handicap. "I'm going to need your help," I say against her lips and she draws back, a sly grin on her face.

Her hands reach for the hem of her sweater, slowly inching it up and over her chest. Her skin is sprinkled with goose bumps and my mouth salivates as she reaches back, her eyes never leaving mine, and unclasps her bra.

Of all the women I've had, though there isn't an overly long list, she's by far the most beautiful. But I knew that before she ever took off her clothes. Inside and out. Skylar is that one rare jewel people don't believe exists and the only one who is rewarded is the person who sought her out knowing how precious she really is.

"Say something," she whispers. There's desperation in her tone. How can she be worried what I think?

"You're beautiful...stunning...gorgeous." If I wasn't half drunk, I'd name all the adjectives and synonyms in the English language for breathtaking.

A slow smile crosses her lips and her hands reach for the hem of my t-shirt. "Let me help you."

My lips refuse to break the kiss and slam back into hers as her hands land on my torso. "I promise next time I'll do the stripping," I mumble between our kisses.

We slowly—and it's not sexy one bit—pull my shirt off, joining hers on the floor.

"Stand," I say.

She gets up on her feet, my face between her legs. Inching forward, I grab her ass with my good hand and thrust her forward. It might not be pretty, but I'm not getting her help to take her pants off.

She moans as her leggings and silk panties pool at her feet, while I savor the scent of her, my tongue swiping for my first taste. A spot that's been taboo between us as friends, is just as sugary sweet as the rest of her. I want to push her into my face, fall to the floor and have her sit on top of me, but tonight, my burning need is to claim her. To bury myself into her while the two of us fall apart in each other's arms.

My tongue slides up her bare stomach, through the valley of her breasts and up her neck until I take her lips with mine, my tongue swirling with hers.

She steps out of her pants, her hands fiddling with the back of my head. I'm so lost in her that it takes me a moment to notice that her hand slides down my stomach, landing on my track pants. Stepping us backward, I lock her to the wall, having to be inventive since I only have use of one arm. I grind into her and she grabs my ass, kneading the flesh with her hands.

She pushes my track pants down and since I went commando tonight, my dick nuzzles into her hot core. She shaved, completely and that fact both surprises and fascinates me. I always assumed she was a landing strip girl, but I'm happy I was wrong. Especially since she's already soaked, and my dick already feels like it's on a slip and slide.

"Sky, you feel so good. So much better than I could have imagined." My lips cascade over her chin, her jaw, the hollow of her neck, as though I'm leaving my scent for any man who tries to take her after me.

Our bodies are hot, wet and sliding along one another as our hands move at a frenzied pace. Damn arm, if it wasn't for that, I'd have her legs wrapped around my waist by now.

Reading my mind, she starts moving us toward the bed.

"Looks like I'm going to take the reins tonight, big guy."

The back of my knees hit the mattress and my butt lands on the softness of her twin-size childhood bed, adorned with pink ruffles and all.

"Don't you worry. One arm doesn't mean I'm down for the count."

I slide up on the bed, wiggling to fit my entire body. She doesn't miss a beat, moving over top to straddle me.

"Condom?" I ask. I can hear the awe in my voice as I look up at the most amazing woman on earth.

"I'm on the pill. Clean?"

"You know it."

She does because part of the Winter Classics medical work-up beforehand means a plethora of tests and we went together.

The real dismay is that my hands can't worship both of her tits at the same time. My good hand greedily takes all it can, moving from one full breast to the other, making sure to give ample attention to both erect nipples.

She guides me in, her hand on my chest, her hair falling behind her back as she arches her neck. There's so much I want to do in this moment. I want to run my thumb down the middle of her neck and follow a path down between her breasts to her center. I want my hands to mold to her hips and guide her gorgeous body back and forth until she's milking my cock.

Sky rides me, and I watch her tits bounce as I do what I

can with my one hand to guide her movements. The only sound in the room is the slapping of our bodies and our mixed cries of pleasure.

When she arches her back and her fingernails scratch down my torso then grip my sides, I know that whatever she's feeling, she's about to come.

I hammer up with my hips to drive into her as deep as I can. My body wants to control the situation, flip her onto her back and thrust inside of her over and over again, but that has to wait until my damn arm is healed.

My gaze fixates on her. Relishing her enjoyment. Enjoyment she's getting from me. This woman who is my best friend, who has stuck by me for four years. Nursed me back to health, brought me into her family like I belonged there all along, and trusts me more than any other person in her life.

She's moaning and chanting my name and something inside of me snaps. Intense pressure swells through my dick, my balls tighten, but she'd yet to come.

I could smack myself for the years I didn't get to experience this moment with her. I'm about two minutes from coming and if she continues to work me like she is, it's going to be more like a second.

"Come, please fucking come," I beg her out of desperation. I can't come before her.

Her gaze falls down to me, and there's a smile on her lips. I use my good hand to bring my thumb to the juncture of her thighs and press down on her swollen bud with my thumb.

She tightens around my shaft immediately. "Oh, Beck," she whispers from her lips at the exact moment I lose my battle and come. She falls on top of me, sliding to the side so she doesn't hit my arm.

She always does think of others.

I brush away her sweaty hair. "I owe you one."

A blissful smile that should make my heart swell, somehow feels like a slash across the tender flesh when it comes over her face. "I can't imagine how amazing you'll be with two working hands."

I slide out from under her, grabbing some tissues and cleaning myself up.

Shit just got a whole lot more complicated.

CHAPTER FIFTEEN

My fist clenches the sheets and my hips buck.

"Fuck," I mumble sleepily, my hand moving down to thread through the dark hair of a girl that's already rocked my world the entire night.

She groans, cupping my balls and I really hope she wasn't down there long before I woke up. It'd have been a shame to miss any of this.

I've never had an alarm clock blow job, but damn if it isn't the best way to say good fucking morning.

She licks up and down my shaft, teasing my balls with her hand as she swallows me until my tip hits the back of her throat.

After sleeping together for the first time, we had sex in the kitchen, I ate her out on the tequila-covered bar, then bent her over the edge of a chair and still my orgasm rushes forward so fast that I can barely contain it.

As if her mouth wasn't enough, she fists the base of my dick, pumping at the same speed as she's sucking me. All the muscles in my body constrict.

"I'm coming," I announce, my eyes focused on the ceiling.

She doesn't relent her steady rhythm, and the ceiling goes black, my mouth dry, from my panting breaths. My entire body feels like a stretched rubber band, and I use every damn trick I have to keep my orgasm at bay, but Skylar just took her finger off the rubber band, and I explode in her mouth, flying high until I'm like Jell-O and lay limp on the mattress.

Moving the sheet from over her head, she lips pepper kisses along my torso, hovering above me so her weight isn't on my arm, and presses her lips to mine. "Good morning."

"That's one hell of a wake-up."

"Want that sponge bath now?" She rolls over, her fingers grazing along my waistline.

"Nah."

I watch her ass when she stands from the bed. "I have to shower. Zoe's coming in a little bit to help me clean up and I don't want to smell like sex."

"It smells good on you," I call out after her.

A big boom from the pipes rattling in the wall when she turns on the water interrupts her giggling.

I sit up in my bed pulling the sheet to my waist on the off-chance Zoe brings Molly and Caiden with her. My phone dings next to the bed, but I ignore it, clicking on the television.

Skylar is in the bathroom, music blaring and the faint sound of her singing along. Last night's events rise in bits and pieces until my sober brain solves the puzzle of what happened last night and the gravity of what that might mean for us.

My phone dings again and I pick it up, ready to send Dax a fuck off text message back. The man thinks it's hilarious to razz me about being injured and whether Skylar's been giving me blow jobs along with her nursing duties. If I try to deny it, he'll know. No one has better hook-up radar than Dax.

But it's not Dax with his smart-ass jokes, it's an alert from Instagram. A shift of energy flickers through the air like a big, dark cloud hovering above the room.

Summer.

Hey, I made the first move. Why am I making the second?

A second message sits immediately under the first.

Saw you at the Classics, you look good, Myers.

The messages continue to beep with the phone in my hands.

You always did make me work hard for your attention.

Message me, if you're back in Cali, let's hook up.

I'm staring at my phone, and my heart beats faster with each message she sends. She always was impatient. Always demanding. Her and Skylar couldn't be more different. But Summer and I share a history that would shake Skylar's solid foundation of a loving family like an earthquake.

"Beck." Skylar stands with a towel wrapped around her torso, another towel twisted in the hair on top of her head.

The smile drops from her lips when she registers the expression on my face and my heart cracks.

"Don't hate me," I say past the lump in my throat.

"Nope. I'm not hearing it, Beckett. Don't you dare say it." She stomps off toward her closet and I rise from the bed and come to stand behind her. She doesn't comment because she already knows I'll follow. I'll always follow her.

Well, not always, not down the aisle.

I lean my shoulder on the wall beside the closet. "I loved last night. Having you after so many years of wanting you."

"Don't even bother saying but," she says loudly to her closet full of clothes.

"But we're so much more than that."

She stands in the middle of the room, drops her towel. "Am I not hot enough for you? You don't want the girl next door type, but would rather some supermodel?"

I swallow deeply, my dick shooting up to full salute.

"That's not it. You're gorgeous and when you consider how many times I was inside you last night you know that's the truth. Hell, look at me now." We both stare at my dick tenting my boxers.

"Don't give me some bullshit about me being your family because if we did cross that line, we'd actually be family."

I shake my head. "Not if we don't work out."

She pulls on yoga pants, no panties and throws on a workout shirt and then a sweatshirt.

"And why wouldn't we work out?" She starts packing a bag.

"Because I'm fucked in the head. Because I'm incapable of having a serious, lasting relationship. I've been by myself for so long...I'll ruin you before you see how I'm not worthy of you. Believe me when I say I'm doing you a favor. I'm a better friend than a boyfriend."

"And how do you know that? Ever since I met you, you never had a girlfriend."

I sit down on her bed and pat the spot next to me. "Come here."

"No." She sits in her desk chair with a corkboard of pictures from her loving childhood behind her. As if it was placed there to make sure to remind me that she's perfect, she grew up with the perfect family and she needs a future with a man who has the same. I know my place in her life and it isn't with matching wedding bands. Even if I wish it could be.

"When I was seventeen, I met a girl named, Summer. We were foster kids in the same home during my senior year. It was the first time I really gave any thought to my future. I had one more year left in the system and I'd already made arrangements to move to Park City and spend every winter riding with the hopes of getting noticed somehow."

She remains silent, so I carry on.

"We were super close. She was having nightmares when she first showed up, so when she'd wake up, we'd sneak out the window and take walks until she calmed down. Eventually we shared stories about what we'd been through. Her story was much worse than mine." I cringe and push my hand through my hair remembering some of what she told me. "We made plans for her to come with me, even though she had one more year of school left after me. I mean, kids leave the system and run away all the time and we figured we'd hide out. Not like anyone would really go looking for her."

She stands up and joins me on the bed.

"Obviously, since hormones control teenager's actions more than their brains, I don't have to tell you what happened. We slept together, and I thought maybe it could work, but it was like a light switch was flipped. She turned into a person I didn't recognize as soon as it was over." I turn to Sky, cupping her cheek in my hand. She doesn't pull away. I've shared a few things about growing up in foster in the past but nothing to this extent. "You have this great family. Your parents, Zoe, Mikey, Chelsea, they'd all protect you from anything. I have you, Dax, and Grady. That's it. Dax and Grady are about a minute from getting married and if I lose you." I push back the tears threatening to fall.

"Beckett," she sighs.

"I can't lose you, Sky. I just can't. You deserve so much in this life and I want to be next to you to experience it, but taking a chance at a relationship, I just...you're asking me to jump out of a plane with no parachute and only a net to catch me below. Who knows if it will support us? It could very well break."

"But it doesn't—"

"Sky, I'd rather have you as a friend than not have you in my life at all." I blink my burning eyes again, praying the tears there don't fall.

She nods slowly, licking her lips. "Okay, we'll forget last night."

"No." I rest my forehead to hers. "I'll never forget last night...ever."

She draws back, covering my one hand with both of hers. "If friendship is all you want Beckett, then you'll need to forget it. I can't say I didn't wish this morning went differently. I love you, and not just as a friend, so I'm asking you to please give me the space I need the next few days. I can only make one promise and that's that I'll try to move past this. I agree I'd rather have you as a friend than nothing at all. But, you're breaking my heart right now."

She stands, picks up the duffle bag she was packing and walks out of the room.

In time, she'll understand I'm doing this for both of us.

I reach for my phone, pull up Instagram and type out a message to Summer.

Don't contact me again. I already have someone in my life who means the world to me.

It's true. There's no room in my heart for anyone but Skylar. Even if I can't be with her.

CHAPTER SIXTEEN

Skylar didn't return until after I had gone to bed that night. Zoe never showed up or any other member of her family. I cleaned up the tequila, the snacks and the rest of the mess with my one good arm and regretted what I'd said to Skylar the whole time. But convinced myself it was the right thing to do. And it was. For her. Regardless of how shitty I might be feeling about it.

Neither one of us might think that after what we experienced last night with each other, but in five years when she's happily married with kids, I'll be the only one left hurting. She'll be happy and loving her life. And at least I'll still have her as a friend.

The following morning, I make us breakfast, and yes, I now realize how much I could've been doing on my own instead of relying on Skylar.

She sits down at the table with a meek good morning while I place her egg white omelet filled with spinach and Parmesan cheese and a side of fruit on the plate in front of her. She's sitting here in her pajamas, her nipples poking out of her tight tank top. I already noticed her short boxers that display the bottom of her ass.

"Thanks." She moves her fork around the plate without picking a piece of food up. "I thought about it and if you want me to move on, I will."

I blow out the breath I'd been holding since I heard her moving around upstairs.

She props one foot up on the edge of the chair, swinging her hair over to one side, leaving one side of her neck exposed. I slide into the chair to hide the chub in my pants.

"So, I think it's fair to tell you that I should be hearing about grad school in the next few weeks. Also, I have a date this afternoon after your doctor's appointment. I haven't decided anything yet about grad school or skiing, so please don't ask. I hope you're right, Beckett." She drops her fork and stares me in the eyes. "I hope you're right. I hope us having sex didn't already ruin our friendship otherwise, what's the point of not exploring us as a couple? I guess only time will tell."

I grab her hand from across the table. She doesn't pull away, but she doesn't grip my hand back, it just lays limp in my hands. "Thanks, Sky, I promise I'm leading us down the right path."

She nods, slides her hand out from between mine and leaves the room. "I need to get ready."

TWO HOURS LATER, a silent Skylar and myself leave the doctor's office with my cut off cast in a bag.

"My arm feels so small."

"It looks smaller. The doctor said you'd have to gain

your strength back." She uses the key fob to unlock the doors to the minivan.

Even without a cast, I look like a schmuck sitting in the passenger seat—the mom missile is just salt in the wound.

"I have to stop at Walgreens. You can stay in the car."

"No, I'll go in with you."

She says nothing and the volume of the music in the car rises and I see she's increasing it on the steering wheel.

I reach forward, turning the knob down. "I think I'm going to catch a flight back to Utah."

We need some time apart to forget all this, so we can go back to being us. In the meantime, I can't sit here and pretend we're good together. I should've never listened to my dick. All I had to do was endure a few more weeks.

"Oh. Okay." She pulls into the Walgreens parking lot, the car about to tip on two wheels, and slams on the brakes seconds before we smash into the building. "I'll be back." She throws the van in park and gets out.

Fuck this.

I follow her into the store, her eyes fixated on the signs of each aisle, obviously, on a mission.

She turns down an aisle and I'm a step behind. She grabs a box of condoms and I reach for her arm.

"Don't do this," I snap.

She yanks her arm away from me, her eyes laced with anger. "You're delusional." Her voice is quiet even though there's no one around us.

"I said I was sorry, damn it."

The two of us stand in the middle of the aisle, our eyes laser focused on one another. "You think those cute dimples as a sorry is going to fix this?" she pokes me in the chest. "That's why you're delusional."

She tries to walk away, but I whip her back around. "Don't walk away from me."

Again, she removes herself from my hold, her arm swinging to her side. "You want to do this here?" She waits for a second and when I don't say anything she continues. "You broke me. Fucking broke me, Beckett." Tears well up in her eyes. "And now a minute after you get your cast off, you're going to hop on a plane back to Park City because you don't need me anymore? Well, I don't have to be okay with it. You aren't the only one who gets to make decisions about us. You don't want me? Fine. Someone else will. Someone else will be the one to fuck me every night. Someone else will have the pleasure of my lips wrapped around their dick. Someone else will give me the pleasure of bearing his child. Someone else will slip a ring on my finger."

"Just fucking stop!" My fists ball up at my sides.

"What's the problem, Myers? Too much detail for you?" She juts out her hip, her face red and flustered.

I hate what we've become, and truth is, if I stay it will only get worse. The only chance to salvage what we have is distance.

"I don't need to hear it, I feel it." I step closer. "I'm broken, too, Sky, but this is best. You have to trust me on this."

"Right now, the sight of you literally nauseates me."

I step back, her words cutting me.

"And for future reference, I don't care how this affects you. Because you caused it. We could be happy, Beckett, but you're choosing to run." A tear slips down her cheek and my body instinctively moves toward her. Her hand lands on my chest, effectively leaving me in the cold. "Book the flight then."

She circles around to exit the aisle the opposite way.

I notice a few lingering stares, but this is Chicago, surely, they're used to this sort of thing?

"Sky? Are you okay?"

You have got to be fucking kidding me. This dipshit again? Does he not work for a living?

"Not you. Not now." She holds her hand up to Ben and walks straight to the cash register.

"What did you do to her?" Ben asks me from the end of the aisle.

I lift my middle finger, turn and follow her like I always do.

"You hurt her," he accuses me as I walk around him.

"So did you."

"But?"

I whip around and surprise Ben. He steps back. "Back off, man. She's moved on. You broke her heart years ago, so go home to Beth and remember *you* made that decision. Skylar's my problem, not yours."

He mocks offense and I roll my eyes then turn to face Skylar who's standing there with her wallet open staring at us.

"I'm your problem? Fuck you."

She pays the cashier, forcefully grabs the bag and flees the store.

"Why are you so twisted about that guy? It was years ago." I'm hot on her heels as we walk toward the van.

She whips around in the middle of the parking lot. "Because it was mortifying! I thought I knew how he felt and then he goes and screws around with my best friend. Can you even process what that would be like? And here I am again...thinking I know how a guy feels about me, but I'm wrong again."

She spins back around and sprints the short distance to where the van is park. Although I'm right behind her, she manages to get into the driver's side, start the engine and lock me out.

I KNOCK. "Sky, you aren't going to leave me."

She puts the van in reverse and I chase it down, pounding on the hood, but she just keeps on reversing until I have to decide if I want to break something else or stop chasing her. I figure she might as well cool off, so I stop, standing in the parking lot, watching her fishtail and drive away from me.

I always knew she'd leave me behind, this just wasn't how I imagined it.

CHAPTER SEVENTEEN

The taxi stops outside Skylar's house and I have to say I'm kind of scared to go in. I don't see the minivan in the driveway, so I take my chances. After paying the driver, I notice the mailman is one house away, so I wait. He hands off the envelopes to me with no you're welcome after I say thank you. Did someone erect a billboard advertising what I did to Skylar? Using the key to go through the front door, the noise inside tells me something isn't right.

I shut the door, take off my shoes and coat, unsure why since I might be running the opposite way in a second. Rounding the corner into the family room, a familiar voice puts my body at ease.

"Fucking hell, he's such an idiot."

Dax.

"Give him a break. It took *you* forever."

Demi.

"Not four years."

Dax again.

"I wouldn't have waited."

Demi.

"Yeah, you would have."

She giggles and I can just picture them snuggled on the couch, him kissing her neck and her smiling, lovesick expressions on their faces. I'm so not in the mood.

"Say you would have."

"No," she squeals.

"Say it."

"Don't go after the nipples."

Oh, screw this, I'm over their cutesy shit.

"I really don't want to see her tits, so..." I walk in and Demi scrambles off Dax's lap, although he easily plops her back down and rests his arm over her lap.

"If it isn't the stupidest motherfucker I know." Dax's razzing voice says he wants to laugh, but he truly does mean it.

I sit down on the chair, tossing the mail on the coffee table, followed by my feet.

"You got your cast off." Demi smiles, and I'm surprised she's being so nice to me.

"Yeah."

We pretend I didn't overhear them talking about Skylar and me. Not that I should be surprised, Demi's Skylar's best friend. I'm sure by now they're all in the loop.

"Why are you guys here?"

Dax's face beams. "It's not every day you turn thirty."

My face pales. How could I forget about that lovely day I was born, when my parents looked at me and said, 'nah, he's not a keeper?'

"You're getting old. Old enough that you should know better. You're making high school decisions bro." Dax taps his head, his eyebrows up.

"And that's my cue." Demi stands.

Dax grabs the waist of her jeans and she falls back down to his lap.

"You know the rules." He purses his lips out for a kiss.

She does that annoying giggle thing again and does as he says. Thankfully, they don't use tongue.

"It's good to see you, Beckett." Demi's hand lands on my shoulder as she rounds the back of the couch and walks out of the room.

"Save it. I'm not in the mood. Actually, I'm booking a flight back to Park City for tomorrow."

"You're gonna run?" It comes out of his mouth like he honestly can't believe it.

"I'm not running, I'm giving her space."

He sits up, his ass on the end of the couch. "Space to what? Hate you more? Plan your murder? Damage is done, dude. That friendship that was so important to you...that went out the window the minute you stuck your dick inside her."

I wince at his words. Honest yet accurate. "Did she put you all on speakerphone and tell you all at once what happened between us?"

"News travels fast in this group. Don't act like you haven't been the initiator of the telephone game a time or two." He raises his eyebrows once more.

Unfortunately, I can't argue with him.

"So, you came here to what? Talk me out of doing the right thing?" I slide to the edge of the chair because what I really want to do is pace the floor. One drunken night's decision and my entire life has blown up like a propane tank in the hot sun.

"No. That's the funny part. She planned your entire birthday party before all this shit went down. Grady and

Mia are on their way here, too. We're supposed to go to a bar tonight. Some VIP crap."

Of course she did. Planned to celebrate a day I've never thought of as worth celebrating. Because that's how amazing she is.

I focus on the wood grain of the coffee table. How the stain is darker in some spots, the scratches that probably came from Skylar and her siblings when they were younger, or maybe they're more recent from Molly and Caiden.

"We're fighting."

He shakes his head. "Of course you are. You fucked her and then told her she was a mistake."

"I said *IT* was a mistake."

"She's a chick. She heard *SHE* was a mistake."

I throw my hands up in the air. Defeated.

He leans back, resting his ankle on his knee. "I get that you grew up in foster care. I don't know what you went through, but my growing up wasn't so great either and I had a biological mother. Think of it this way, at least you don't have a daily reminder that she's only interested in your money."

"Still?"

"Every day since I cut her off."

"You did?"

He loses the gleam that was in his eyes seconds ago. "I gave her twenty grand and said not to call me for money again. Guess she didn't completely understand the direction because she says she gave my brothers some." He holds his hands out. "Those are my demons and I've slashed away at them, so I can be in a healthy relationship."

"How much Dr. Phil have you been watching?"

He laughs, but there's no real humor to it and his eyes narrow. "I could sit here and lecture you, but the truth is, you gotta find it in yourself. The fight for her. You run from anything but snowboarding. Last month you stood in my room and listed off reasons why I needed to go after Demi. Why my upbringing wasn't the whole of who I was. So." He slides forward on the couch again. "Look on the bright side, you've got me." He winks. "And just so you're aware, I'm not some consolation prize, okay?"

I laugh, shaking my head.

He stands and leaves the room. I inhale a deep cleansing breath. Picking up the mail to put it on the counter where Sky's parents usually keep it, I walk it over to the box in the kitchen.

I drop it in right before the return address flashes up. *University of Chicago.* I scramble to pick it back up, holding it up to the light to see what it might say. I think I see welcome and congratulations, but I can't really be sure. She applied and that means she's serious about leaving skiing for good. I have a feeling my trip back to Park City will be on my own, whether I like it or not. Which is fine, we're both better off that way anyway.

CHAPTER EIGHTEEN

Chelsea got us more connections. Did her entire college class go into the bar industry?

We've gone to dinner, Skylar on one side of the table, me on the opposite. I couldn't even tell you why the both of us have agreed to go through with this party. She obviously hates me now. From the death stares sent my way by Chelsea and Zoe, you'd think my face was on America's Most Wanted.

Walking up the stairs and through the roped off VIP section, Demi and Mia sit down, their conversation hushed, but their eyes shooting in all different directions.

Dax heads to the bar, ordering a round of shots while Grady disappears into the bathroom. Mikey's already on the dance floor with some random chick he picked up on the way up the stairs. Seriously, that guy is a magnet. Chelsea must have a thing for bouncers because she's flirting with one at the edge of the roped area. Vin and Zoe watching the dance floor like it's foreign land they're not familiar with. Skylar, my Skylar, sits wearing a tight blue dress and heels with her hair pinned up.

Her words, 'you broke me' haunt me each time our eyes skim along one another.

"Drink up, birthday boy!" Dax shoves a shot glass into my hand and then moves along, passing out shots to everyone. "To my best buddy. Here's to women, beer and song. May they never be flat. Happy birthday, asshole! I fucking love ya."

I roll my eyes. The girls laugh. All except Skylar whose face is devoid of emotion.

We all tip the shots back.

"Let's go dance," Chelsea says to Skylar, gripping her hand.

"Sure." Skylar lets Chelsea lead her to the mass of people grinding and sweating on the dance floor.

I'm lost in the memory of our dance only a week earlier. How her body molded to mine like we were statues fit together. How soft her skin was. How good she smelled.

Grady comes alongside me, tipping his shot back and sliding the glass across the table. "This shit has got to stop. Your birthday is as much fun as a fucking meeting with my accountant."

"Yeah, I can only do so much entertaining before I'm going to want to be paid." Dax laughs.

"We might as well live it up. We're here, it's your birthday," Grady says.

I look over my shoulder, seeing Skylar's first smile all night. She's enjoying herself, so maybe I should try to as well.

"Another round." I head to the bar.

You'd think I learned my lesson about drinking where Skylar's involved, but I guess I'm still working with my high school brain like Dax said.

The guys and I drink a few more shots. Pretty soon

we're taking some pictures, laughing about nothing. Dax and I get into a meme war on Instagram then I drunkenly try to explain the game Zoe brought over for games night. It's like the three of us from before the Classics, before they found girlfriends. The only thing missing is Skylar, who would usually come up and join me in the fun.

Demi and Mia stay on the couch sipping their drinks and chatting. Probably planning their double weddings or some shit.

I'm busy posting something I shouldn't to Instagram when my message light pops up.

HEY IT'S LUCA. **What bar r u guys at?**

LUCA, Luca, Luca, who is he? The name is familiar, but I can't place it. He must know me though, so I hammer back a message and tell him where we are. He'll never get in because hello, the line is around the corner and we're in VIP. Good luck, Luca, whoever you are.

We take a couple more shots, but I have a feeling Grady isn't taking his because he's still standing straight whereas I have to keep holding the edge of the bar to steady myself.

Skylar returns from the dance floor, sipping a bottle of water and joins the girls on the couch. She purposely tries not to make eye contact with me. The girls embrace her in what looks like congratulations. Their excited smiles and the way they're practically bouncing in their seats tells me she told them the news. She's going to grad school.

They're happy for her, you selfish bastard. Why can't you be?

I feel like I'm at war with myself.

"Myers!" someone screams my name and I look up to see a guy. He looks familiar.

Skylar turns and looks, a smile forming on her lips. She stands, walking over to the bouncer, placing her hand on his arm and pointing to the guy who yelled my name.

Then I see who's with him and my drunken brain finally makes the connection.

I head over, placing my hand out in front of me. "Hey."

"You cool if we join you?" Luca asks, shaking my hand.

"The more, the merrier, of course, but your brother can leave." I look over his shoulder at that shithead Mauro cozying up to Skylar.

He chuckles. "Sorry, man." He cringes but says nothing else.

"Isn't there another Bianco?"

"Sucker had the late shift." He glances over to Grady and Dax, his eyes widening. This guy must really follow snowboarding. Half the time I forget I'm a professional snowboarder that people might recognize. It's not like we're Kris Bryant and Anthony Rizzo walking around Chicago.

"Oh, hey." I nod over to my friends who are back in deep discussion, most likely about my sorry ass, and wave them over. "This is Dax Campbell and Grady Kale. Guys, this is Luca."

They nod, shake hands. "Want a drink?" Dax asks.

"Hell yeah," Luca responds.

The three of them talk shit. Well, Luca asks them a million questions they're more than happy to answer. My eyes set on Mauro and Skylar, talking. She's laughing, her finger twirling her hair, her cheeks flushed with pink. So, this is what it'll be like watching her with another man she seems to like.

My throat feels like it's closing in and I swallow past the growing lump.

"Hard to watch, huh?" Chelsea asks.

I glance over at her, nod and turn my gaze away.

"It's not too late, you know."

"Give it a rest, Chels. Will everyone just fucking give it a rest?" My voice is louder than I would've preferred.

"Whoa, buddy." Grady raises his eyebrows, silently questioning if I'm okay.

"I'm fine. I'm fucking fine."

A few more heads turn.

"It's okay if you're not." Chelsea's smug smile is prominently on display.

"I am," I bite out.

My eyes land on Skylar, who is staring at me, questions in her eyes. Questions she would've asked me last week. Questions it seems she doesn't care to ask anymore.

"Beck," Mia says, placing her drink on the table, about to stand up.

I put my hand in the air. "Everyone just fucking leave me alone."

All the tension locks up in my body like I'm in a suit of armor and can't move.

"Hoff," Dax comes to stand on the side of me, using the nickname that usually calms me. It's a nickname that someone took the time to make up for me. It put me into their club and I've never minded being razzed for being a Cali skater and the shit comparison to Baywatch or David Hasselhoff. In my world as demented as it is, if you tease me, you like me. It's not true on the schoolyards these days, but in my world a nickname means respect. It means you belong.

But it doesn't work this time. I'm too far gone. Weeks of pretending I don't want Skylar followed by finally having her and then having to give her up has brought me to my limit.

"I can't." I choke out the words and I might not be able to see Dax, but his body stiffens next to me.

She stays on the opposite side of the small VIP section next to the douchebag rather than check on me. But I deserve it. I selfishly took her when she wasn't mine to take.

"Let's go." Dax's hand cups the back of my neck to guide me out of the bar.

I shake him off, stalking across the room, over top of the glass coffee table in front of the couch until I'm standing right in front of Mauro, looking down at Skylar.

"I get that I fucked this entire thing up, but you sure are moving on fast."

An empty laugh tumbles out of her mouth. "You only got one part correct there, the part about you fucking up."

"You knew my issues."

Mauro puts his hand on my chest to keep me from stepping forward, but I twist and push it off me.

"This is the only way." I sound like I'm pleading. "I wanted to keep you in my life."

"You could have had me." Her voice hiccups, tears welling in her eyes. "I gave you time. More time than anyone else would have." She swipes the tears from her eyes.

"Guys." Grady's in between us now, but I step forward, pushing him away from us.

"Why can't we just go back to being friends?"

She throws her arms up in the air. "Because in the end, you'll ruin me. I can't do it anymore, Beck. We've come to a crossroads and either you jump on the train with me, or I have to leave you at the station. It's as simple as that."

"Looks to me like the train already left."

"Oh, my God." She shakes her head, looking at all of our friends. "Get out of my face, now, Beckett. I can't. I just can't. I need to be away from you."

"So you can fuck him?" I thumb to Mauro, her words barely processing in my alcohol-soaked brain.

"No!" she screams.

Now we've caught the attention of the bouncers and they're heading in our direction. Demi and Mia are suddenly at her side, tears are cascading down her cheeks, smearing her perfect makeup.

Someone grips my upper arms from behind.

"There's no need for that. I'll get him out," Dax says and the bouncers, I assume, let me go.

I run to Skylar, my hands planting on her cheeks, my lips pressing against hers. Our tongues glide and my stomach lightens as if the boulder I've been carrying around is being turned to dust. I sprinkle a few last kisses to her lips and rest my forehead against hers. "I do love you. You'll forever be the one who got away."

A fresh set of tears fall to the floor between us. She shakes her head. "I didn't slip out of your grasp, you shut the door in my face." Her hands leave my body and my skin chills.

She walks away, and I watch her back until someone taps my shoulder.

I circle around, but I'm blindsided by a fist against my cheek.

"Sorry man, but you know you deserve it."

I cradle my cheek, the pain dulled a bit from the alcohol.

"Nice, Vin." Grady helps me to my feet, shoots a look to Mia. "I'll see you back at the house?"

"Yeah, maybe you guys should head to a hotel."

"Definitely a hotel," Dax says.

CHAPTER NINETEEN

I wake up alone. In a bed foreign to me with a cold bag of water next to my face.

Sitting up, I see that I'm still in the t-shirt and jeans I was wearing last night. I check my phone and see no missed calls. Then I glance at the clock.

Fuck.

I stand up, searching the small-ass hotel room to make sure I have everything.

Wallet, check.

Phone, check.

Dirty clothes, check.

Morning breath, check check.

Rushing out of the hotel, luck is on my side because a taxi is waiting outside. I hop in and give Skylar's parents' address.

In the car, I rest my head against the cold window, having to piece little chunks of time together to make sense of everything that happened last night. I kissed her. A smile creases my cracked lips. Vin punched me. Good for him. I'm sure I deserved it. My fingers gently touch my cheek. It's still sore and probably black and blue. I haven't bothered to look in a mirror yet. I know we screamed at one another. In the middle of a bar. Her tears, freely flowing without a care who saw her. It's so not Skylar to lay herself out there like that.

I wince at my actions and how much I drank. It was my thirtieth, but I should've limited my alcohol consumption. I had too much turmoil inside. Something was bound to snap.

The taxi stops in front of the house and I pay the man and make my own walk of shame up the concrete path to the front door.

I ring the doorbell. Me using a key after what I've done doesn't seem right.

"Hey," Demi answers, her hair askew, her pajamas still on.

"Is she here?" I walk into the house that doesn't hold that same warm feeling it did weeks ago. These people hate me, just like her now, and I have the black eye to prove it.

"No. I think she's at her sister's."

I head up the stairs and pack up my room. I'm done taking a shower early enough to catch my flight. I stand in the hallway, staring at her childhood bedroom door.

Fuck this.

I open the door, stepping into her personal space one last time. I pick up a few pictures tacked to the corkboard above her desk. Her easy going, soft welcoming smile can be found in every picture. She always did steal the room when she walked in.

Sitting down in her chair, I find a piece of paper and a pen, hoping to make the sting of what happened between us less hurtful. She has to know the truth. That I've loved her since the first time I saw her, I was just too chicken shit to admit it. How lucky she is to escape the coward I am. But hopefully she understands I never meant to shut her out, or to hurt her. That I was sheltering her from a part of me that's as foreign as a rainforest is to her.

I place the note on her desk, stand and dig out my key to the house, putting it down on top, then tuck her desk chair back under the desk. Moving to the bed, I know I'm intruding. She doesn't want me here, but I lift her pillow to my nose and inhale the scent of her. Closing my eyes, I let the smell of vanilla wash over me. I put it back exactly how she had it and put my duffle bag over my shoulder, closing the door behind me.

"Leaving?" Dax asks, shirtless with athletic shorts showing off way more than I want to see.

"Yeah. Make sure she's okay?"

"We're sticking around for awhile. Demi's trying to really piss off her mom by staying away as long as she can." He chuckles, but his lips go firm. "You sure this is what you want?"

"I've overstayed my welcome. It's too late."

"It's never too late for a stud like you."

A tight smile I don't feel tips the corners of my lips. "It is."

I shake his hand and do a one arm hug.

"Hey, let's get together soon. Plan a guy's trip." He shakes his head. "Did I just say that shit?"

A real laugh flows out of me now. "Yeah, you did, but it's on."

We stand in the foyer looking at each other for a minute.

"I thought I heard you. You going to Park City?" Grady walks down the stairs, fully showered and clothed.

"Yeah, my flight leaves in a few hours."

A honk outside signals that my Uber is here, so I grab my suitcase, give Grady a one arm hug. "Tell Mia I say bye."

"Will do."

The two of them stand on either side of me, finally not trying to convince me to change.

I open the door, stepping back out into the mild air. It feels like true spring is just around the corner. With one last wave to my friends, I put my luggage into the trunk of the Uber and climb in.

"O'Hare Airport."

The guy nods, shifts into drive, checks his mirrors a couple of times before he starts to pull away from the curb. Did he just get his license? Let's fucking go. He slams on the brakes and my head stops inches before the headrest.

"Are they coming?" he asks, looking over at the house.

"Nah," I say, turning to look when my door opens and a shirtless Dax slides in.

"Come on. The weather might've warmed up, but this is Chicago for fuck's sake. My balls are shriveling up."

I slide across the seat—why, I have no idea.

The other door opens and in hops Grady.

"Okay, guys, I'm squeezed like a hot dog in here."

"Bad analogy, Hoff," Grady says, taps on the headrest. "You can go."

The driver listens to the person who isn't going to pay him and turns his wheel to get out of the parallel parking position.

"Get out of the car," I say.

"I wanted to let your sorry ass leave. I really did," Dax says. "I'm so exhausted with your bullshit, believe me. You're ruining my high of getting laid on a constant basis. Seriously, I thought I was a nympho, but Demi, man, I'm barely keeping up."

"Thank you. Thank you for that piece of information."

"It's the perks of a relationship. Am I right, Grady?" He looks past me.

"I have no complaints." Grady shrugs.

"If this is your 'go buy Skylar a ring campaign because I'll get laid all the time,' I have some information for you. It won't last. Sooner or later, you're not going to be as attracted to her. She's going to see you lying around, not doing jack-shit and she'll be rolling over leaving your sorry ass."

She'll figure out you're not good enough I don't add. Or maybe that's only true in my case.

He circles his finger around his face. "She'll never deny this gorgeous mug."

I roll my eyes. "Thanks for the pep talk guys, but we can chat about this another time." I glance at the time on the car display. "I have a flight to catch."

"Told you. Waste of fucking time." Dax speaks his mind openly to Grady.

"Hoff, it was my idea to jump in the car—"

"Captain obvious, I'm not wearing a shirt."

Grady shakes his head at Dax's interruption. "If you get on that plane, shit, you're already so deep in that hole, man. As your friend, I can't in good conscience let you ruin your life."

"I'm not—"

"You fucking are!" He raises his voice, so much so that the Uber driver grabs his cell phone and puts it in his hand. Like he'll call the cops if need be. Where was he last night when Vin flattened me like a fucking pancake?

"I know I had a happy childhood. Shit, my parents live and breathe for me. Brag about me, worry about me. And Mia's got that too."

"Thanks, I feel so much better now," I deadpan.

"You're going to live your life alone because two crappy, careless people who happen to have gotten together one night and fucked, screwed you over before they even knew how awesome you are? You're not them. You don't even know who the hell they are. Nor do I think you care. So, *why* are you letting the fact that they left you thirty years ago ruin your life now? I get that you have issues. I get you're worried that she's going to wake up one day and be like, who the hell is this jackass I married?"

"Marriage." Dax cringes. "You're pulling out the big guns there."

"Dax," Grady sighs.

"You spent all this time keeping your distance from her because you were scared you'd lose her, but look, Beck, you lost her despite all that. Do you really think she'll ever be your friend again?"

I say nothing as the Uber pulls into the airport.

"She won't. Sure, you'll have to see each other at mine and Dax's wedding."

"Whoa, whoa, whoa." Dax holds his hands up in the air. "Let's not throw my name in the mix."

Grady tilts his head because we both know Dax might walk down that aisle before Grady. Dax's silence and the way he's rolling his eyes says we're right.

"Baby showers, barbecues, hell in a couple years we'll all be back at training and competing," Grady continues on with his lecture. "You might be cordial, but the friendship you had, it died. So, you can get on that plane..."

The car stops, and the Uber guy turns around, seeming enthralled with Grady's inspirational speech.

"And leave her behind—"

"Or you can fight for her," the Uber driver adds.

"Exactly," Grady agrees. "Because, Beckett, you're

always too busy pointing the finger at yourself. How screwed up you are, but after this, Skylar's the one who thinks she's screwed up. She's thinking for some reason *she's* not good enough for *you*."

"Thanks for that." I pay the Uber driver on my phone leaving him an extra few dollar tip for having to listen to these two ramble the entire ride, then nudge Dax to get out.

"Nope. Make the right call here."

Dax looks to Grady for some sort of advice. "Let him go, Dax. You're right, it's hopeless."

Dax sighs, opening the door and stepping out.

"Excuse me, Sir, you cannot come into this airport without a shirt or shoes," an attendant screams, running over to us.

"Well, this has been eventful. Have a safe flight buddy. Text me when you land." Dax pats me on the shoulders, hopping back into the car as I walk through the sliding doors.

Out of Chicago and out of Skylar Walsh's life.

CHAPTER TWENTY

I go through all the motions...check-in, checking my baggage, security and finally buying a coffee to wake my ass up before I collapse on the germ-infested vinyl seats and miss the announcement of my flight boarding.

I'm boarded and in my seat, which I upgraded to first class because I need something in my life to not suck right now. The flight attendant comes by, but I decline anything. All I want is sleep and the promise that this shattered feeling inside will stay in Chicago and disappear when the plane's tires land in Utah.

First class is empty, probably because the ski season is done for the year. The tourists start to dwindle before there's another rush in late spring and summer for golf, horseback riding, and fishing. It's really perfect timing for me to return since I'll have a few weeks to keep a low profile.

Sleep evades me. I try to picture my life without her in it and it just seems like a vast wasteland. Maybe we were always headed for this moment—the point of no return. Perhaps even if we hadn't slept together, push was eventually going to come to shove. Everything I did to make sure she'd remain in my life one way or another seems futile now.

Grady's voice rings loud in my head.

Am I really leaving her with scars?

This entire time I was worried about her leaving me, and what it would do to me. It'd strip me bare if I put it all out there and she rejected me. But she was there for my taking, ready to jump in with both feet and I'm the one who left her all alone. I was the asshole. I acted like my own fucking sperm and egg donor. *I* made her feel like I've felt my entire life.

"Fuck!" I yell.

"Is there something wrong?" The flight attendant walks down the aisle to me and bends down to speak with me.

"How much longer until we land?"

She glances at her watch. "Probably an hour or so."

"Shit. Any way we can land this thing?"

She laughs, her perfectly shaped eyebrows rising. "Um, no."

Worth a try, unless I want to feign a heart attack or something. "Then how do I get a ticket to board the next flight back to Chicago after we land?"

She scrunches her forehead and sits down next to me. "Are you on the wrong flight?"

This isn't some Home Alone bullshit and with how many times you have to show your damn boarding pass it has to be nearly impossible for that to happen, doesn't it?

"No, I have to get back to Chicago."

A smile forms on her lips. "A girl?"

Okay, I'm over the advice column shit now. The light bulb over my head is finally on and could act like a light-house if I wanted.

"Yeah," I say sweetly with the hope it might earn me some romantic brownie points and score me a ticket at not triple the cost. Not that Skylar's not worth it, but it just means there's less I'll have to spend on her.

"Okay, let me find out for you." She stands up.

I take the phone from the headrest, punching in her cell phone.

Voicemail. Shit.

"Sky, please don't go out with Mauro. I'm coming. I'm sorry. I'm a fucktard. Please, please, this is the last time I'll tell you to wait for me. I promise."

I end the call, the flight attendant handing me a glass of scotch.

"Nah, just anything with caffeine. Alcohol, me and this girl don't mix."

She laughs, taking her scotch back with her but I swear she chugs it down before she moves past the partition.

"Okay," she says when she returns, handing me a soda. "This plane will be heading back to Chicago after refueling and clean up. You have to get off, buy your ticket, and then you can re-board. Give me your luggage tags." She holds her hand out.

I dig in to find the luggage tags in my wallet and hand them to her. She heads back up to the front and gets back on the phone, returning a minute later.

"You're all set. Now it's just a waiting game."

The minutes tick by like hours. Could I really not have figured this out while still in the airport?

An hour later, the tires land in Utah. I do everything the flight attendant told me and I'm surprised how smoothly it all went. I couldn't get first class, so I'm sandwiched between a mom with a baby and a business guy on the return flight, but I'm not about to complain.

"Sorry to both of you, but there's a lot of calls about to be made."

They each just stare at me, so I swipe my credit card and pick up the phone. Organizing everything I need for tonight. When I land in Chicago, I won't be coming to her, she'll be coming to me. That is if Demi and Dax can stop fucking for ten minutes to do what they're supposed to.

If I'm going to jump, I'm doing it with both feet and no parachute. What better way is there than to go big. Big always is better.

CHAPTER TWENTY-ONE

The lights of the Chicago high rises light up the dark room, windows showcasing the view from edge to edge, thirty stories up in the air with the bustle of people below.

I gulp down the lump in my throat and shift trying to get more comfortable. My shirt is too stiff around my neck. The tie too suffocating. The jacket too restrictive. I miss my track pants and t-shirts, but Skylar is worth wearing this thing for the rest of my life.

"I don't understand. Why are we here?" Skylar's voice is faint.

"You know Dax, always impulsive. He wants your opinion about this place in case he buys the condo."

"What? Why would he buy a condo? It is a nice area." Their heels click on the hardwood floor. Lights flicker on in each room. "I thought you guys were thinking about staying in Vermont?"

"Well, family issues and all."

Demi sure sucks, I can even tell she's lying.

"What'd we miss?" Grady walks in.

"Oh, I love the view of the lake," Mia gasps. I hope Skylar does too because it cost a small fortune to get a lease on it with such short notice.

"Maybe we should move to a city," Grady says.

My head falls back in exhaustion. If she doesn't step in here soon, my heart is going to stop.

"Nah, I'm a Vermont girl. Plus, neither of us would survive in a place we can't strap on our boards and ride."

"True. I need the snow," Grady agrees.

"Chicago has snow," Skylar says.

"No fucking mountains though." Dax's voice joins the group and the door shuts. "Seriously, that neighbor guy is nosey. I don't think this is the place for us, babe."

"Yeah, I agree. We sure will miss you, Sky, but we'll visit often."

"I'll visit, you'll visit. It'll be fine...why are you leaving? Aren't you going to at least look at the bedrooms?"

"Oh, I guess." Demi must turn back around. Dipshits can't put together a plan to save their lives.

Lead her in here. They have one fucking job. Okay, well more than one, but this is the most important.

The light turns on above my head, shining down on the sprinkled red rose petals scattered across the wooden floors.

They shut the door behind her and Skylar turns, walking over and placing her hand on the knob. Her hair is thrown into a ponytail and she's wearing yoga pants, gym shoes, and a hoodie. She's never looked more beautiful.

The fact she's not pounding on the door to escape is a good sign.

"It's too late," she says to the back of the door.

"Please just listen to me. One last dinner and if you want to leave me, I won't stop you."

She turns, and her gaze shifts to the small table set in

front of the window with takeout Chinese food containers and chopsticks along with two bottles of water.

She bites down on her lower lip, her eyes never reaching mine. "If I sit down and eat, you'll let me go then?"

"Yes."

"A half hour. That's it." She walks to the table, sits down and crosses her arms over her chest. "Why are we eating in the bedroom?"

"Because I had to make sure you wouldn't run."

She cocks one eyebrow at me. "Of the two of us, I'm not the runner."

"True." I sit down across from her. "Hungry?"

"Nope."

"Did you get my message?"

"Nope."

"Missed call?"

"I didn't miss it."

I knew she'd be hard, but either I don't know her at all or I'm a bigger douchebag than I realized. I guess it's the latter.

"Sky, I'm so sorry."

She holds her hand out to me. "Stop. I'm done with the sorry. If you can't handle a relationship more than friendship, I've decided I don't want either. I'm not sure what all this is about, but it's over, Beckett. We had a nice run. Friendships die all the time."

"Yeah, they do and ours died. I'm not here to earn your friendship back, Skylar."

She stares blankly at me.

"I'm here to win your heart. I understand it won't be easy. I understand if you never want to talk to me again, but that's why we're here. This condo is mine. If you're in Chicago, I am too. I mean I'll have to travel, otherwise, I can't afford this place. So, during qualifying and training, I'll have to be in Park City, but we'll make it work. Somehow. It doesn't matter."

"What makes you think I'm staying in Chicago?"

"I saw the letter. I saw the girls congratulating you."

She shrugs in an 'okay, you have a point.'

"Anyway—"

"Why do you think I'd still see you even if you are here?"

Her position hasn't changed. She's closed off and I can't say I blame her. I used to be the same way. Until she taught me a better way.

"I'm hoping with enough begging you will."

Another shrug and she crosses her arms in front of her chest.

"I know you don't want to hear I'm sorry, so let me try to phrase it differently. I want you. I *need* you. I could sit here all night and grovel for you to accept me back into your life. To take the chance and move on, but honestly, there's only really one thing I want to do tonight."

"What's that?"

I fall to my knee, opening the ring box that holds the engagement ring I bought after I landed. I pop open the box and her arms fall to her sides.

"No, Beck. Don't."

"Now, Sky, is that the story you want to tell our grandchildren one day? That I fell on bended knee and you told me to get up?"

Her lips tick up but quickly fall back straight.

"Don't do this just to keep me in your life."

I leave the ring box on the table, sliding across the floor, clearing a path through the rose petals. "You are so special. You've always been special. It's always been you. The one who taught my battered heart to trust and to love. See, Sky, I grew up always feeling like I wasn't worth sticking around for. I was so worried you were going to find out what an idiot I was. That I wasn't worth your time. That'd I mess this up somehow, and the fact that I made you feel that way..." I run a hand through my hair. "This ring isn't because I want you in my life. I mean, I do, but I'm not proposing to you because I think I have to. I want to cherish you, nurture you, start a family, and make a home together because if we're going to do this, we're going all in. We already know everything there is to know about one another. We're putting everything on the line, all our stakes on the table and I'd never bet against us because me and you, we're meant to be together."

I blow out a breath after my declaration, hoping my rambling made halfway sense.

"Ask me again?" she says, her voice soft.

I dare a smile and pluck the ring out the box. The two-karat pear shape diamond sparkles on the silver band. It's simple and elegant and suits her perfectly.

"Skylar Walsh, will you please marry me?"

She looks at the ring and purses her lips. "I have three conditions."

I chuckle. "Sure."

"Do you, Beckett Myers, promise to never run away again?"

"Only if you're chasing me with a butcher knife."

She nods. "Do you, Beckett Myers, promise to never have to say sorry to me again?"

"Well, I could, but I'd hate to start our life with a lie. I'm gonna fuck-up, you know that."

She nods, accepting my answer.

"Last condition, Beckett Myers. Do you promise to

never rent or buy a piece of housing without talking to me first?"

"Why? This is perfect. The university is right over there."

She drops to her knees and places her hands on my cheeks. "I'm not sure why we need to be by the university when I'll be skiing in Park City."

"What?" I pull back, wide-eyed.

"I'm not retiring. Not yet."

"Shit, I guess I need to sublet this place." I shake my head. "It doesn't matter. Sky, will you be my wife? Put me out of my misery."

She holds out her left hand and I place the ring on it, the fit perfect. I'll have to thank Mia for sneaking into her room to scour her jewelry box and find her ring size.

"All right Myers, you're mine."

"No, you're mine." I smash my lips to her mouth and she giggles as we fall to the floor.

It might've taken me forever to get here, but with Skylar in my arms, I can't be upset because I ended up exactly where I should've been the entire time.

EPILOGUE
SKYLAR

Four Months Later...

I stand in front of the mirror, my white dress puffing out into a million layers, my bodice beaded down to my waist.

"I still say you should've planned it like most people do. This whole whirlwind wedding stuff is a lot." Chelsea sits down on the couch, her blue dress shining and complimentary to her skin tone. "And I know you say I'll wear this dress again, but I'm calling bullshit, I won't. And you'll never wear the one I made you wear."

I'm surprised Chels is bringing up her brief but volatile marriage since she always seems to prefer to pretend like it never happened.

"Note taken, but I have to say, mine is ten times more beautiful than the pink number you put me in."

I continue staring at myself in the mirror. Surprised I'm here. Surprised it's Beckett. Surprised my last name will be Myers. Well legally, not professionally. I gotta win that gold with Walsh, it means something.

"Your groom is ten times better, too."

"I won't fight you on that. He's slow out of the gate, but he sure knows how to make up ground."

"That's where I went wrong. Mine was fast out of the gate and then didn't know which lane he should stay in."

I laugh then grow quiet, checking off a mental checklist in my mind and making sure everything is taken care of. "Why did we rush again?" I ask, my nerves getting the better of me.

"It wasn't a rush. It was four years too late." Demi saunters in, my veil in her hands. Her eyes catch mine in the mirror. Neither her or Mia was upset in any way that I beat them to the altar.

"Thanks," I whisper.

"You know I can't lie." She laughs and positions my veil perfectly on top of my head. "Rumor has it that Vin threatened Beckett that if he runs, he'll cut his balls off and then his dick inch by painful inch."

"That's some real Dexter shit. Make sure I never get on his bad side." Chelsea grabs a glass of champagne.

"No baby though, right?" Chelsea asks *again*. Demi frowns in the mirror probably wondering why my cousin is giving me so much shit before saying I do, but I don't care. I should've done the exact same for her.

I assumed she was happy. I assumed he treated her right. I'll never assume anything again.

"No baby," I say, shaking my head in amusement.

And there won't be until after the next Classics. One, because it might just put Beckett over the edge and two, I want time with my husband, just the two of us.

"Okay, let's go, let's go, let's go! Your groom is looking hot up at that altar. Not as hot as my man, but he won't stand up there forever." Mia holds up her long matching blue dress as she walks into the bridal room.

Yeah, he will.

My parents walk in while the girls are telling me how beautiful I am and how wonderful Beckett is. Reconfirming that I'm making the right decision.

"Thanks girls, I'll see you in a few."

They file out and my parents—who aren't in the loop on what happened four months ago between us—still think Beckett is perfect, as they should, and are happy to welcome a new son-in-law into the family.

"You look beautiful, sweetie." My mom steps forward, gripping both of my hands in hers. "Your dad and I just wanted to make sure you're ready for one of the biggest decisions in your life. We know you and Beckett have known each other for a long time, but a four-month engagement..." She continues, but I've heard it over and over again for the past four months. Why couldn't I give her a nice long engagement where she could plan for four hundred guests, a seven-course meal, and book the most spectacular place in Chicago?

Beckett was adamant though, that he wanted me as his wife right away. I think that fear that he's not worthy still lives inside of him a little, but he's yet to admit it. Hopefully, in time, that fear will wither away and die as I smother it with love.

"Mom," I say, and she stops her rambling. "I love Beckett and he loves me. There's no baby on the way. There are no citizenship issues. There's no pressure on either of us to marry the other. We love each other and we want to be legally bound, that's all."

She squeezes my hands, appeased with my answer. "Okay, I'll see you down there. Your brother is already halfway in the bag and he has to walk me down the aisle before standing next to Beckett. I love you."

"I love you."

She leaves the room and I release a breath knowing my dad isn't going to ask me questions. He knows I'm making the best decision. He knows Beckett is the only one for me. I'm pretty sure he thinks of him as his son already.

"Remember, you're always a Walsh." He holds out his arm to me and I slide mine through his.

"I know."

It's hard to give up your name, a name that's been a part of you for so long. I jokingly asked Beckett one night if he'd take my name. Yeah, that was a hard no. It's his last connection to his parents, whoever they are. Although I hate them as much as he does, I can't help but wonder if he would've turned out differently if his story were different. If my parents would have left me in front of a fire station when I was barely out of my mother's womb, I don't know how much self-worth or how trusting I'd be with people.

We round the corner and the music starts. Molly and Caiden start their walk up the aisle and Caiden dips his hand into the basket his sister is carrying to throw the flowers. Molly slaps it. Caiden cries. I never expected the perfect wedding.

I catch a glimpse of Beckett through the church stained window at the top of the aisle, dipping his own hand into the basket and handing some to Caiden while he talks to Molly. Zoe glances back at me, a smile on her lips.

Yeah, I'm a lucky girl.

By the time I'm standing at the entrance to the church, Beckett's eyes are completely on me, the love he feels pouring out of them. That love was always there, but it was clouded over with fear. It's now there, shining through in its purest form and as I step forward toward him and crinkle the letter he gave me that I've wrapped around the bottom of my bouquet, I don't regret the heartbreak we put each other through because it was our enduring love that brought us to this moment.

Skylar,

Four years ago, I sought you out. You were such a nice person you never noticed how I hung around every time you went to the bar or the cafeteria at the village. I was drawn to you, your friendly smiles and kind words. I can't explain it, it was this pull you had over me, and it was soul deep. Once I had the smallest bit of your attention, I only craved more. Over the course of the past four years, you've made me a better person. You're the first person who could make me forget about my past and the burden I used to carry on my shoulders didn't feel so heavy anymore. In your eyes, I'm someone who is worthy of you. Sometimes, falsely, I lose myself and believe that to be true as well. I'm sorry about last night. I'm sorry for ruining what we had, but honestly, I never deserved you to begin with.

I'm heading back to Utah today. I wish you the best in grad school and I'll miss you on the team. I know my opinion probably means nothing right now, but Skylar, you're an amazing skier and the sport will be losing something special if you retire. Just think about it. It's one decision you can't turn back on.

The time we spent together was some of the best in my life and there will be a persistent piece of me missing without you by my side. But my wish for you is that you find true happiness and the person who makes you feel the way you've always made me feel...like anything is possible with that person by your side.

Love,
  Beckett

MY EYES WATER as I think of the words he wrote to me that day because I did find that someone. And he was here with me all along.

When Beckett takes my hand as my father passes it over, he squeezes it and smiles, and I have no worries about our future together. We'll ride through the peaks and valleys together as one, just like we always have.

The End

COCKAMAMIE UNICORN RAMBLINGS

Beckett…tough case, right?

Friends to lovers is always a tricky road to go down, both in real life and in fiction. Because once you've crossed that line there really is no going back. In Beckett's story, we wanted to be sure to convey that he wasn't a manwhore who didn't want to settle down with only one woman, rather he was afraid, fearful that he wasn't good enough for Skylar and fearful to risk losing her from his life for good. Piper had to work her magic to weave in that fact throughout the story and we know at times you probably wished you could rip Beckett's balls off and shove them down his throat you were so frustrated with him. Believe us, we were too. But we believe we were true to Beckett's character and that it would take more than one smack on the head for him to realize the catch he was. I mean, hello, there's only so much fiction we can put into a story and men are not known for their stellar insight toward women. 😊

Skylar, oh sweet Skylar. We'd like to believe that even through Beckett's voice, you saw her vulnerable side. A little unlike the Skylar that was in On Thin Ice, we know, but sometimes you're more vocal when you're protecting your friends, than yourself. I think we can speak for not only women, but men too, that there's a time when you're a little disappointed over how something you put so much effort into turned out. Winning bronze put Skylar into a zone to reevaluate her life. She loved Beckett—he was the guy she loved and waited for. He's not always worth it, are we right? But Beckett was for Skylar.

This entire series was so fun to write and although they were long novellas we like to believe they packed a punch. Although the Olympics and Winter Games are over by the time you read this, the gang is sure to pop back in our future books.

As with any of our books, without the following people, we wouldn't be able to do what we love.

Letitia from RBA Designs

Ellie from Love N Books for line editing.

Shawna from Behind the Writer

Social Butterfly PR

All the bloggers who carved out time to promote us and/or read and review the book. Thank you for selecting us to read when we know you have so many options. We're very grateful for the support!

All our early ARC readers, for wanting to get your hands on our words as early as possible. You keep us going.

And of course, all our unicorns. We could put on repeat what we've written in the back of every book. You are what keeps us going with fresh ideas and new characters. Your enthusiasm for our works makes those long days and nights in front of a keyboard worth it.

We're sure you faithful Unicorns saw the hints of a new

series in the works and a few new characters who need to find that special someone. Do you need to go back and read? Who do you want to find a HEA? Let us know!

Xo
    Piper and Rayne

ABOUT PIPER & RAYNE

Piper Rayne is a USA Today Bestselling Author duo who write "heartwarming humor with a side of sizzle" about families, whether that be blood or found. They both have e-readers full of one-clickable books, they're married to husbands who drive them to drink, and they're both chauffeurs to their kids. Most of all, they love hot heroes and quirky heroines who make them laugh, and they hope you do, too!

Bedroom Games

Cold as Ice

On Thin Ice

Break the Ice

Box Set

Hockey Hotties

My Lucky #13

The Trouble with #9

Faking it with #41

Sneaking around with #34

Second Shot with #76

Offside with #55

The Greenes

My Beautiful Neighbor

My Almost Ex

My Vegas Groom

The Greene Family Summer Bash

My Sister's Flirty Friend

My Unexpected Surprise

My Famous Frenemy

The Greene Family Vacation

My Scorned Best Friend

My Fake Fiancé

My Brother's Forbidden Friend

The Baileys

Lessons from a One-Night Stand

Advice from a Jilted Bride

Birth of a Baby Daddy

Operation Bailey Wedding (Novella)

Falling for My Brother's Best Friend

Demise of a Self-Centered Playboy

Confessions of a Naughty Nanny

Operation Bailey Babies (Novella)

Secrets of the World's Worst Matchmaker

Winning My Best Friend's Girl

Rules for Dating your Ex

Operation Bailey Birthday (Novella)

The Modern Love World

Charmed by the Bartender

Hooked by the Boxer

Mad about the Banker

The Single Dad's Club

Real Deal

Dirty Talker

Sexy Beast

Hollywood Hearts

Mister Mom

Animal Attraction

Domestic Bliss

Charity Case

Manic Monday

Afternoon Delight

Happy Hour

Blue Collar Brothers

Flirting with Fire

Crushing on the Cop

Engaged to the EMT

White Collar Brothers

Sexy Filthy Boss

Dirty Flirty Enemy

Wild Steamy Hook-up

The Rooftop Crew

My Bestie's Ex

A Royal Mistake

The Rival Roomies

Our Star-Crossed Kiss

The Do-Over

A Co-Workers Crush